A Stranger in the Neighborhood

Nick turned down the volume on his radio, the Yankees already ahead 3–2 in the third inning, a commercial break in progress, and rolled off his bed. He went and stood by his window, looking down from the sixth floor to the street below as day dropped into night. He could hear the TV going in the living room from Amelia's show. His mom would be in her room reading, he guessed. Soon his father would be on his way home from work, his train pulling into the station near the Stadium.

When Nick looked down to the street now, suddenly he felt all the air rush out of him.

There was a man standing on the corner near a lamppost, halfway up the block across the street.

Nick was sure the man was staring up at him, or maybe he was imagining it. A million thoughts crossed Nick's mind at once: *What if he's watching me? What if he's here for my family? What if he works for ICE? What if . . .*

Nick slowly stepped back from the window, closed the shade, and got back into bed. He reached over to the radio on his night-stand and turned up the volume on the game. The Yankees were about to come to the plate in the top of the fourth.

I'm home, Nick thought. *So why don't I ever feel safe here?*

BOOKS BY #1 *NEW YORK TIMES* BESTSELLER MIKE LUPICA

Travel Team

Heat

Miracle on 49th Street

Summer Ball

The Big Field

Million-Dollar Throw

The Batboy

Hero

The Underdogs

True Legend

QB 1

Fantasy League

Fast Break

Shoot-Out

Last Man Out

Lone Stars

No Slam Dunk

Strike Zone

Triple Threat

THE ZACH & ZOE MYSTERIES:

The Missing Baseball

The Half-Court Hero

The Football Fiasco

The Soccer Secret

The Hockey Rink Hunt

The Lacrosse Mix-Up

The Hall of Fame Heist

MIKE LUPICA

STRIKE ZONE

PUFFIN BOOKS

PUFFIN BOOKS
An imprint of Penguin Random House LLC, New York

First published in the United States of America by Philomel Books, 2019.
Published by Puffin Books, an imprint of Penguin Random House LLC, 2020.

Visit us online at penguinrandomhouse.com

THE LIBRARY OF CONGRESS HAS CATALOGED THE PHILOMEL BOOKS EDITION AS FOLLOWS:
Names: Lupica, Mike, author. Title: Strike zone / Mike Lupica.
Description: New York : Philomel Books, 2019. | Summary: Twelve-year-old Nick
García dreams of winning MVP of his summer baseball league, of finding a cure for his
sister, of meeting his hero, Yankee pitcher Michael Arroyo, and of no longer living in
fear of the government and ICE agents. Identifiers: LCCN 2019014207 |
ISBN 9780525514886 (hardback) Subjects: | CYAC: Fiction. |
Dominican Americans—Fiction. | Family life—New York (State)—New York—Fiction. |
Baseball—Fiction. | Bronx (New York, N.Y.)—Fiction. | U.S. Immigration and
Customs Enforcement—Fiction. | BISAC: JUVENILE FICTION / Sports &
Recreation / General. | JUVENILE FICTION / Sports & Recreation / Baseball
& Softball. | JUVENILE FICTION / Social Issues / Emigration & Immigration.
Classification: LCC PZ7.L97914 St 2019 | DDC [Fic]—dc23
LC record available at https://lccn.loc.gov/2019014207

Puffin Books ISBN 9780525514909

Printed in the United States of America

3 5 7 9 10 8 6 4 2

Text set in Life BT.

This book is for
Conor Gleason of the Bronx Defenders.
A hero of the city of New York.

1

IT FIGURED THAT NICK GARCÍA WAS PLAYING IN THE DREAM LEAGUE.

He loved to dream as much as he loved throwing a baseball, something Nick knew in his heart—even if he'd never say it out loud—he could do as well as anybody his age in the South Bronx.

Nick's coach, Tomás Viera, once told him he could throw even harder at the age of twelve than Nick's hero, the great Yankees pitcher Michael Arroyo, had at the same age.

"Now, I can't actually prove that," Coach Viera said. "But I saw Michael play when he was in Little League. Heard the sound the ball made in the catcher's glove. The sound you make is louder."

Back when Michael Arroyo was growing up in the Bronx, he'd pitched on the north side of 161st Street, right where they'd built the new Yankee Stadium. At that time, it was the baseball fields of Macombs Dam Park. Once the new Stadium went up, a replacement Macombs Dam Park opened on the south side of 161st, in the footprint of the old Stadium. This was where Nick and his teammates on the Bronx Blazers now practiced and played, often with fans filing past on their way to Yankee games.

"I know about the fields where Michael Arroyo pitched," Nick told his coach. "I've seen the old pictures online."

"You seem to know just about everything about him," Coach Viera said.

It was true. Nick dedicated a lot of time to finding out every-thing about Michael, including what happened during his child-hood, when he came to America on a boat from Cuba with his father and brother. He'd read every news piece, biography, and article in existence, not to mention the ESPN documentary he'd seen about a hundred times. Nick even knew about the time Michael threw a ball from home plate to center field at the old Macombs Dam Park to stop a purse snatcher. It wasn't just Michael's fame that drew Nick's attention. Michael represented everything that was possible for Nick to achieve. Seeing a brown-skinned kid from the South Bronx, just like him, make it onto the Yankee mound one day was enough to keep Nick fixed on his dream.

"Someday," Nick told his coach, "I'm going to make it across that street and pitch for the Yankees."

They were sitting on the grassy hill behind home plate, both having arrived early for tonight's practice.

Coach smiled and pointed over to their left, where the Stadium loomed so big that sometimes Nick imagined it blocking out the sun, or swallowing up half the South Bronx; its shadow casting over the corner bodegas and fruit vendors on the street.

"It's right over there," Coach said, like it was simple. "Only a couple hundred yards."

"Or a million miles," said Nick.

"Michael Arroyo made it there from 158th and Gerard," Coach Viera said. "You can make it from 164th and Grand Concourse."

He grinned as he pointed to the word printed on the front of Nick's blue practice T-shirt: "Dream."

"It'll take a lot more than that," Nick said.

"Ah," Coach said. "But I honestly believe the good Lord has blessed you with a right arm like Michael Arroyo's left."

"Michael is special."

"So are you," Tomás Viera was quick to say. "And this summer, it could be you standing on his pitcher's mound."

The Dream League was part of a larger organization, run by Major League Baseball, called RBI, which stood for "Reviving Baseball in Inner Cities." This August they were holding a summer league tournament for teams from the Bronx. It was arranged in partnership with the Yankees that the MVP of the tournament would get to throw out the first pitch before a Yankee home game.

Nick had already been named the MVP of his RBI team in the spring. If he could somehow manage to do it again, he'd get to know, for one moment, what it was like to be in the middle of the most famous field in the world. Then it wouldn't only be the people in the stands watching him, but perhaps Michael Arroyo, too.

A lot needed to go right for that to happen. Nick had to pitch his absolute best in the summer league, the same as he had in the spring, and the Blazers would have to win the tournament—he was almost sure of that. For the most part, in sports, the MVP came from the championship team.

But at least the chance was there, to make it from this field to the one across the street.

"Can I ask for a favor?" Nick said to his coach.

"Go for it."

"Let's not talk about the MVP award. I don't want anybody to think I care about it more than winning the tournament."

"Oh, I know that," Coach said, with a wave of his hand. "And so do your teammates."

"But can we please just not talk about it?" Nick pleaded, swiping a palm over his buzz cut.

"I won't if you don't want me to," Coach Viera promised.

"Not gonna lie, it would be great to throw out that first pitch," Nick said, punching a fist into his mitt. "But I'm not fixed on that."

He was.

Nick wasn't going to admit it to his coach, or his teammates, or even his parents. He was too embarrassed to tell any of them how much it would mean to throw that pitch. How much he wanted it.

But he did.

Coach Viera got up and made his way down the hill and across the sidewalk embedded with small plaques that told of great moments in Yankee history. By now, some of the other Blazers were starting to arrive for practice, which was scheduled for six o'clock sharp. With Coach Viera, you started on time and you ended on time.

Nick stayed where he was another minute, looking around at the Stadium to his left and the elevated subway tracks in the distance. He listened to the thrumming of the trains pulling into and out of the station at 161st Street, a sound that was as much a part of his life as the cheers echoing from inside Yankee Stadium.

Nick loved this field the way he loved his neighborhood. Even the racket from the cars on the Major Deegan Expressway, crawling along in both directions at rush hour.

"Sometimes I think," his mother, Graciela, would say, "if you could move your bedroom to that field, you would."

"And you'd still be telling me to keep it clean," Nick would reply, sending the two of them into a laughing fit. Then she'd pull him in for a long hug.

There was no Yankee game tonight, as the team was in Toronto finishing out a long road trip against the Blue Jays. So it wouldn't be one of those nights when Nick and his teammates could hear the game being played across the street. Usually, they could tell immediately if something good, or maybe even great, had just happened for the Yankees.

Nick had been inside Yankee Stadium a few times. His father tried to take him once a year. They usually sat in the bleachers, because those were the only tickets Victor García could afford. But even from there, in the most distant part of the ballpark, Nick thought the view of the game was beautiful. His father would always take pictures to remember the experience, but as much as Nick liked having those pictures, he didn't need them. Long after the game was over, he could vividly recall the memory of everything he'd seen, both in his mind and in his heart.

Alone on the hill, about to make the walk down to the field, Nick closed his eyes. This time, he wasn't envisioning those games from the bleacher seats.

No.

Instead, Nick García pictured himself going into his big windup, the one he'd copied from Michael Arroyo even though

Nick was right-handed. The one he practiced alone in his bedroom in front of the full-length mirror, bringing his leg up high and rotating his right arm forward.

He put himself right there in the center of the Stadium, throwing that first pitch.

Nick knew that people who threw the ceremonial first pitch usually just lobbed the ball in to avoid the embarrassment of bouncing the ball in front of the plate or throwing it wildly over the catcher's head.

But it would be different if he got the chance.

If he made it over there, he would bring the heat.

But only if he *did* make it over there. Only if he was still living in their apartment on Grand Concourse, just a few blocks from where Michael Arroyo grew up. Only if his family wasn't deported first. Nick was an American citizen because he was born in America. So was his older sister, Amelia. His parents, however, were not. If they were sent back to the Dominican Republic, Nick and his sister would go with them.

Even for a kid with big dreams like Nick García, that would be a nightmare.

"HEY!"

The voice made Nick jump. But then, it didn't take much to startle him. It could be something as ordinary as the sudden blare of a car horn, and Nick would still jolt.

But he relaxed as soon as he saw the faces of his two best friends looking down at him: Ben Kelly, his catcher on the Blazers, and Diego Gomez, the team's center fielder.

"You shouldn't sneak up on a guy like that," Nick said.

"You shouldn't be taking naps before practice," said Ben, combing his hand through a thick mess of curly red hair.

"I wasn't taking a nap," Nick shot back. "I was just thinking."

Diego shook his head, bringing his slender light-brown arms into a stretch behind his back. "That can get you into trouble."

"Oh yeah? How would you know?" said Ben.

"Hey," Diego said. "I think about stuff sometimes."

"Oh yeah? Like what?" Nick said, joining in.

Diego scratched his head, as if confused. "Hang on, lemme think . . ."

"What about you?" Ben said to Nick. "What were you having deep thoughts about this time?"

"The usual," Nick said.

Both Ben and Diego knew what the usual was. He'd told them

everything about his family's situation. And they were well aware of Nick's fears.

"Just remember," Ben said, "no matter what happens, we've got your back."

"Even when you're sneaking up on me from behind it?"

"We weren't sneaking up on you!" Diego said earnestly. "We just thought you were trying to get some beauty sleep. Even though you'd probably have to sleep longer than that Rip Van Winkle dude for it to work on you."

"When you *are* thinking," Ben said to Diego, "does it ever occur to you that you might not be as funny as you think you are?"

"Never!"

Nick had known Ben and Diego since kindergarten, but they first became friends on the baseball field. Over the years, they had grown to be as close as brothers. So even though Nick wasn't the type to share personal information, he knew he could trust them with anything. That's how they knew Nick's parents had come to the United States on tourist visas from the Dominican Republic when they were in their early twenties. Almost from the moment they arrived, Victor and Graciela García knew they wanted to make their home in America, and set out to secure jobs to establish themselves in a new country. However, this also meant that they were undocumented immigrants. Even though Nick's parents both held steady jobs and paid taxes and Nick and his sister attended public schools in the Bronx, Victor and Graciela García weren't American citizens.

Nick's dad had always taught him that America was a country built and defined by immigrants coming from all corners of the globe. But now many of the people running the government, including the president himself, viewed immigrants as some kind of threat to America, no matter what country they came from. It was the reason why Nick and his family lived in fear the way they did.

"For the next couple of hours," Ben said to Nick, "how about we all just worry about baseball? You down with that?"

His thick red curls always seemed to be flying off in every possible direction. They framed his freckled face, with skin as white as a brand-new baseball.

"I am *so* down with that," Nick said. "Now help me up."

He reached out with his right hand, and Ben pulled him to his feet. The three of them walked down the hill toward the field. And with Ben on one side and Diego on the other, Nick felt as safe for now as he possibly could. Sometimes it seemed as if baseball was the only thing with the power to do that—though he knew that the game he loved so much could never protect him from the government, especially if the government ever came for his family.

What was the expression?

"Safe at home"?

For the next two hours, he would let baseball make him feel that way. People in the league always talked about what great control Nick García had when he was pitching.

They had no idea.

Baseball was about the only thing in his life he *could* control.

Except he had none today.

Control.

While the rest of the Blazers went through infield and outfield drills, Nick and Ben went to the far field at Macombs, the one clos-est to the subway tracks, so that Nick could pitch off a mound. It was what the big-league pitchers called a "throw day," to prepare for his first start in the tournament. Coach had told him to take it easy—not to throw too many pitches and, most importantly, not to throw as hard as he would in the Blazers' opener.

But once he and Ben were finished soft-tossing, Nick had no feel for the ball in his hand, no idea where it was going once he released it. So it didn't matter how hard he threw. If Ben set his mitt up outside, Nick threw the ball inside. If he wanted the ball low, Nick threw it high. There were pitches in the dirt, and times when Ben had to come out of his crouch and nearly jump to keep the ball from flying to the backstop.

And the more frustrated Nick got, the harder he threw, even though he'd been warned not to by his coach. The kid who prided himself on being able to put the ball wherever he wanted couldn't come close today.

Heat?

Right now, he was only making *himself* hot.

Nick had never pitched more than five innings in any of his spring games. His old coach, Mr. Contreras, had put him on a strict pitch count to protect his arm. From the time he'd first started Little League, none of his coaches allowed Nick to throw curve-balls, under the notion that breaking pitches put too much stress on a young arm. Oh, he would take something off his fastball occa-sionally, even if he didn't think it was very much fun. Sometimes he'd throw a changeup, just to keep batters off-balance.

But the thing that Nick loved most about being a baseball

player was his ability to throw a fastball. It made him feel powerful. Diego liked to joke that they should make him stand a few yards behind the pitcher's mound, just to give the batters a better chance.

He hardly ever walked anybody. It only happened twice during the spring season. Nick had that kind of arm. Sometimes it felt as if the ball he was throwing to the catcher was practically on a string.

Just not right now.

Ben didn't say anything, even though he could clearly see Nick's growing frustration every time he missed his spot. He was counting pitches the same as Nick was, knowing that Coach Viera didn't want Nick to throw more than thirty per session. But by the time he'd finished, maybe only ten of them had been strikes. Possibly even fewer than that.

Usually, no matter what was happening in his life, Nick could focus on baseball when he was on the field, could keep things simple: ball, mitt, strikes.

Then strike*outs* once the games started.

But tonight his pitches mostly resembled the way his brain felt, as in: all over the place. Silence filled the space between Nick and Ben as they walked slowly back to their own field, until Ben broke the ice. "Everything okay?"

Nick managed to curl his lips into a smile, even though he didn't feel much like smiling at the moment.

"You're only asking me that because you're probably wondering if I'm still right-handed," Nick said, attempting to make light of the situation.

Ben shrugged.

"Not an answer," he said.

"I'm fine," Nick replied, a little too quickly.

"Really?"

"You know the deal." Nick sighed. "Always a lot going on."

Off to their left, they saw Diego make a great over-the-shoulder catch on a fly ball Coach Viera hit to him. The rest of the Blazers cheered as Diego threw the ball back to the infield. Then, in typical Diego fashion, he bowed grandly, tipping his hat to reveal a crop of dark brown hair. The kid acted as if there were a spotlight on him at all times. And as the tallest guy on the team with the biggest personality, he couldn't go far without being noticed, so it worked out perfectly for Diego Gomez, who never seemed to have a care in the world.

Nick desperately wanted to feel that way. And wondered if he ever would. On or off the field.

"Is there anything new going on that I don't know about?" Ben prodded.

"Are you serious?" Nick said. "You know me better than I know myself. You knew I didn't have it today after five pitches."

"Why I asked."

"I'll figure it out. Maybe it's good that I'm getting the wild stuff out of the way before our first game."

"No secrets?"

Nick shook his head. "Not from you."

They walked over to the bench near first base, and each took a swig from his water bottle. It was almost time for batting practice.

"My mom always tells me that things work out the way they're supposed to," said Ben.

"She should tell that to ICE," Nick muttered.

Ben swallowed hard. "Did something happen?"

"Yeah," Nick said. "It did."

The word always sounded so innocent when Nick said it out loud: "ICE." Like the cubes you drop in a glass of water or lemonade. But Nick knew better. There was a rhyme he always carried around inside his head: "ICE, not nice."

It stood for Immigration and Customs Enforcement. These were the people who could force you to leave the country if you did something wrong. The ones who could steal your life away from you. Just a few days ago, Nick overheard his parents in the kitchen after they thought he'd gone to bed. They were talking about how two ICE agents had shown up at the home of Mr. and Mrs. Romero, who lived at 170th and Grand Concourse. The men took Mr. Romero to a detention center in New Jersey because he'd once been arrested for driving without a license. Nick heard his mother say that it was a blessing Mr. and Mrs. Romero's sons were grown and living on their own, so at least they didn't have to see their father get arrested that way. But Nick understood what she really meant. If ICE ever came for Victor García, she wouldn't be able to prevent her children from seeing it happen. Because like Mr. Romero, Nick's father had once been arrested for a minor offense, and that sometimes made it feel as though they were living under a microscope. It was like a never-ending chess game, waiting for ICE to make their next move and praying it wasn't checkmate.

Nick quietly told Ben about Mr. Romero, practically at a whisper even though no one was around to hear them.

"Oh, man, that's rough," Ben said.

"Tell me about it."

"Doesn't mean it's going to happen to your folks," Ben said.

"Doesn't mean it isn't," Nick said, feeling the full weight of his words.

"You know what grown-ups say, though. You can only control what you can control."

"Really?" Nick said. "Try telling that to my fastball tonight."

Finally, the rest of the Blazers jogged off the field to get ready for batting practice. Coach Viera was a star pitcher at George Washington High School in Washington Heights before he hurt his arm senior year and lost any chance at getting drafted in the big leagues. It was another reason why Coach was so conscious of protecting Nick's arm. He knew from personal experience how everything could change with a single pitch.

But even though he didn't have much arm left, Coach Viera loved pitching batting practice. Nick went first tonight, spraying line drives all over the field. After his turn, he ran out to second base, which he played when he wasn't pitching. He used to play shortstop when he was younger, but Coach Viera didn't want Nick making long throws from there, so he moved him to second, where he had the shortest throwing distance to first base.

Coach stopped for a quick water break while Diego took his practice swings, and Nick found himself peering down at his glove. His old, beat-up glove.

His mom always offered to sew the laces for him whenever another one would tear. But that was happening more frequently these days, and they both knew she couldn't continue mending it forever. Nick thought back to how excited he'd been when his parents first bought it for him—a Michael Arroyo model. They'd left it under the Christmas tree when he was eight, covered in shiny red paper and a big gold bow. But Nick knew what it was immediately, without even having to unwrap it. It was a little big on him at the time, but his dad promised he'd grow into it. Nick remembered the feel of the leather on his hand for the first time and how hard he'd worked to break it in the right way.

Now it wasn't only broken in; it was falling apart one lace at a time. Nick knew he needed a new one. His parents knew he needed a new one. But it wasn't something Nick ever chose to discuss with them. He understood, without his parents having to say a word, how tight money was in their house, and it never felt like the right time to ask. Not only that, they had other, more important expenses to take care of first.

Namely, his sister's medical bills.

Amelia often needed medical care, and that care cost money. So that meant that, for now, there wasn't enough left to buy a new baseball glove for the family's baseball star.

As Coach came back to the mound, Nick pounded his fist into the pocket of his glove, angry with himself all over again for being selfish enough to think about wanting a new glove with everything else going on. And for wanting to make it across the street to throw that first pitch as badly as he did.

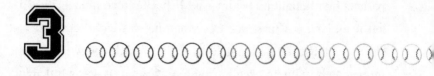
DIEGO'S FAMILY LIVED ON WALTON AVENUE, NEAR THE BRONX County Courthouse, which meant that of the three of them he lived closest to Yankee Stadium. Diego always said the Stadium was big enough to be the sixth borough of New York City.

"The baseball borough" is what Diego liked to call the Bronx.

"What about the Mets?" Ben said. "They're in Queens."

"If you're a Yankees fan," Diego said, "they might as well be playing on the moon."

Nick and Ben dropped Diego at his building. Ben's was next, a block down from Nick on Grand Concourse.

"You watching the Yankee game later?" Ben asked.

"Watching or listening," Nick said. "Depends on whether Amelia's watching one of those *Bachelor* or *Bachelorette* shows."

Nick didn't care for those shows, but he knew his sister did. So he never minded going to his room and listening to the Yankees on the radio instead. At least that's what he told himself. Fighting with his sister over the remote wasn't exactly high on his list of priorities, and anyway, Nick always tried to find little ways to make his sister happy.

Mostly, though, he wanted her not to have a disease called lupus.

When Amelia was first diagnosed two years ago, Nick's parents explained to Nick how lupus affected the body, trying to put in the simplest terms what it meant to have an autoimmune disorder. They told him it was when some parts of your body fight against other parts. In Nick's mind there was no winner in a fight like that, just one loser: his sister.

But Amelia was strong, and always stayed positive, even when her symptoms were at their worst. She even talked about how she had "Selena Gomez disease," because it had come out in the past couple of years that the singer had lupus, too.

"It must mean I'm special," Amelia told Nick when she found out, "having the same disease as someone as glamorous and famous as Selena Gomez."

"Spoiler alert?" Nick told his sister. "You're way more special than she is."

In response, Amelia had raised her hand to the back of her head and posed like a supermodel, and the two of them burst out laughing.

Ever since he found out about Amelia's diagnosis, Nick continued to read up on lupus in order to understand it better, and what it was doing—or might do—to Amelia. The thing that scared him most was that Selena Gomez's lupus had caused damage to her kidneys, enough that she needed a transplant.

The doctors had assured Victor and Graciela García that they didn't think Amelia's form of lupus would ever require something as drastic as a transplant. But sometimes Amelia would be so weak she would stay in bed for days on end. Other times, she would get rashes on her bronze cheeks. Despite these challenges, she had already decided to become a doctor someday, and help people with illnesses like hers. Even after missing several days of school this year, she still ended eighth grade at the top of her class, and was on schedule to begin high school with the rest of her peers.

By now Nick knew that one of the reasons Amelia had to stay inside so often was because too much sunlight contributed to her rashes. That seemed to Nick as cruel as any part of her disease, just because his sister loved being outside so much. But sometimes she stayed in by choice. The rashes made her a bit self-conscious, and she hated getting stares from strangers.

At least the rashes would always go away, eventually. But what never went away were the family's medical expenses. Nick didn't fully understand how health insurance worked. His mom said they went from one short-term plan to another, which was all they could afford. Their options, when Amelia's lupus got bad enough, were community health centers in the Bronx or urgent care clinics where Victor and Graciela could pay in cash. Or, if it ever came to it, the emergency room at hospitals funded by the government. The same government that had them living in fear.

"I don't know how you handle everything," Nick had said to his father a few days earlier.

Victor had smiled, put an arm around his son, and said, "God gives the heaviest burdens to the strongest backs."

Victor García was a man of great faith. He and Graciela were raising Nick and Amelia to be the same. But sometimes Nick wondered about his own faith, and why God had them living in a place where they felt unwanted, fearing the future instead of looking forward to it.

Amelia was on the couch when Nick walked in from practice. Their mom had come home early from her housekeeping job in

Lower Manhattan and fixed Nick and Amelia an early dinner. Later, she would heat up a plate for Nick's dad when he got off his shift at the restaurant where he worked in Midtown.

Amelia looked up from the TV at her brother as he walked into the living room.

"Excuse me," she said, as if she were a news reporter. "Aren't you the star pitcher for the Bronx Blazers?"

"The way I pitched tonight," he said, flopping down onto the couch beside her, "you must be confusing me with someone else."

"Oh no!" she said, putting the back of her hand to her forehead dramatically. "Was my little brother less than perfect?"

"Good thing it was only practice," Nick replied. "The way I was lobbing the ball all over the Bronx, I wouldn't have made it through the first inning in a real game."

"But it *wasn't* a real game," she said, kicking him from underneath her blanket.

"Is that supposed to make me feel better?"

"Yes!"

"Then stop kicking me."

"No!" she said, kicking harder, with both feet this time.

They laughed, and Nick was glad she was feeling well enough to tease him this way.

"How is it," he said, "that you're always the one making me feel better when that's supposed to be my job?"

"Is it because I'm so very, very *special*?" she said, both of them knowing she would never actually say that about herself.

"You *are* special," Nick said. And he meant it, too.

"Yeah, yeah, okay. Well, if I'm special, then so are you."

"Being able to throw a baseball doesn't make you a special person," he said. "Just a special player. Not that I felt like one tonight."

She put a hand on his knee and gave him that serious older-sister look. "We're both going to get through everything we need to get through."

He looked at Amelia and once again felt the guilt rise up in his chest. He was placing far too much emphasis on a baseball tournament and a prize that wouldn't do anything to make things better for Amelia or the family.

"Let's change the subject," he said.

"To what?"

"How about . . . *The Bachelor*?"

Amelia howled with laughter. "Puh-leez, you don't care about *The Bachelor*. Isn't there some baseball game you want to be watching?"

"I'm going to listen to it in my room," he said.

"You don't always have to let me watch the TV, you know."

"Yeah, but I like listening to baseball on the radio," Nick said. "It's fun to imagine what's happening based on what the announcers are saying."

Amelia wasn't buying it, but she didn't press. "Is your man pitching tonight?"

They both knew she was talking about Michael Arroyo.

"Not till the weekend," Nick said.

"See—look what he went through," Amelia said, "and now he's playing for the Yankees. One bad day isn't gonna stop you from getting where you wanna go."

Nick rubbed a hand over his neck. "I keep telling myself that."

"At least nobody thinks you're lying about your age," Amelia said.

Nick nodded knowingly.

Michael Arroyo didn't have a birth certificate when he'd fled Cuba with his father and brother, just a document from his baptism for identification. By the time he took Little League by storm, some refused to believe he was only twelve years old, and tried to get him kicked out of the league. But that wasn't the worst of it. Back when he was trying to pitch his team into the championship, Michael's father passed away, leaving him and his older brother, Carlos, living on their own. Losing both their parents was hard enough, but to make matters worse, Michael and Carlos lived every day in fear of being separated or put into foster care by child protective services. Nick could relate. Even if he didn't find himself in the exact situation Michael had as a boy, Nick feared ICE would tear his family apart the same way Michael's nearly was.

"He went through a lot, for sure," Nick said.

"Not only did he survive it all," Amelia said, "he ended up fulfilling his dream."

Nick snorted. "It means he was lucky *and* good."

"You'll get there," she said. "I have faith."

The remote for the TV was on the small side table at the end of the couch. Nick picked it up and handed it to his sister. "I hope you're right," he said, and headed for his room.

The Yankees were waiting for him in there.

NICK GARCÍA KNEW HE LIVED IN A WORLD WHERE YOU COULD WATCH baseball on a laptop or even a cell phone, if you had one good enough for that, which he didn't. Instead, he carried an old flip phone that had once belonged to his father. Nick's parents thought it was important for him to have a phone, so they could reach him in case of an emergency. Though most days it burned a hole in his pocket. The last thing Nick wanted was to get a call about Amelia or to find out something had happened to his dad.

So Nick couldn't carry baseball around in the palm of his hand like some of the guys on his team could. With the MLB app, they could watch any game they wanted at the touch of a screen, anytime, day or night. But that figured, Nick thought. There was an app for practically everything. Nick wished there was one that could remove all the pressure from his life so the only thing he had to worry about was throwing a strike when he needed one.

But there was just something about baseball on the radio that he liked, even if he had the option of watching any game he wanted to. Ben and Diego teased him that listening to games on the radio was something old people did, but Nick didn't care. He *liked* lying on his bed at night, window open, the sounds of the game mixing with the sounds of the street below. Sometimes he fantasized about sitting in the booth with the Yankee announcers,

John Sterling and Suzyn Waldman, broadcasting the game along with them. He could even hear himself making John Sterling's home run call about balls being high and far and gone.

Whenever Michael Arroyo was pitching, Nick would try to guess whether he was about to throw his fastball, his curve, or his changeup, depending on the count. Then he'd close his eyes and picture Michael making the motions before delivering the ball to the plate.

Maybe it was silly, but Nick felt connected to Michael. It wasn't just that he looked up to him, but he felt like Michael would understand what Nick was going through. The part of Michael's story that Nick loved the most was how a great Yankees pitcher known as El Grande Gonzalez had become a hero in Michael's life. Like Michael, El Grande had made it across the Florida Straits, escaping Cuba during a time when that was near impossible due to strict laws.

Not only did Michael pitch in the new Yankee Stadium now; he was married to El Grande's daughter, Ellie.

Nick turned down the volume on his radio, the Yankees already ahead 3–2 in the third inning, a commercial break in progress, and rolled off his bed. He went and stood by his window, looking down from the sixth floor to the street below as day dropped into night. He could hear the TV going in the living room from Amelia's show. His mom would be in her room reading, he guessed. Soon his father would be on his way home from work, his train pulling into the station near the Stadium.

When Nick looked down to the street now, suddenly he felt all the air rush out of him.

There was a man standing on the corner near a lamppost, halfway up the block across the street.

Nick was sure the man was staring up at him, or maybe he was imagining it. A million thoughts crossed Nick's mind at once: *What if he's watching me? What if he's here for my family? What if he works for ICE? What if . . .*

Nick slowly stepped back from the window, closed the shade, and got back into bed. He reached over to the radio on his nightstand and turned up the volume on the game. The Yankees were about to come to the plate in the top of the fourth.

I'm home, Nick thought. *So why don't I ever feel safe here?*

The man on the street was gone by the time Nick's dad got home from work at ten thirty. Nick knew because he had peeked outside after turning off his lights for the night. Even though it was summer and Nick didn't have to worry about getting up for school in the morning, bedtime for him was always set by the last out of the Yankee game. On nights when they played on the West Coast, the games would go into the early hours of the morning. Nick would stay up as late as he could before drifting off to sleep, and either his dad or mom would come in to turn off his radio.

"I have good news," Victor García said when he came in to say good night. "I may be able to catch most of your game on Thursday. Unless they change my schedule, but I should be working the lunch shift that day."

Nick brightened, but just as quickly reeled in his excitement. He knew how hard his dad worked for the family, and didn't want to get his hopes up. "If they do change your schedule, it's okay," Nick said. "I mean, I want you there, but I'd understand."

"Nothing makes me happier than seeing you pitch," his dad said, sitting on the edge of Nick's bed. "When you're on that mound, I feel as if everything's right in the world."

"Except it's not." Nick considered telling his dad about the man on the street, but decided against it. What good could it do? It would only make him worry, and that was the last thing his dad needed right now.

"Someday it will be; I'm convinced of that," his dad said. "I have always believed that your mother and I are here for a reason. And I will never believe that reason is for us to be asked to leave."

He stood up, then leaned down to plant a kiss on Nick's forehead. As he did, Nick caught the familiar smell of the restaurant still on him.

He closed his eyes, trying not to think about the Official People who might be out there waiting for him like they had once been for Michael Arroyo.

Maybe even on the street where Nick lived.

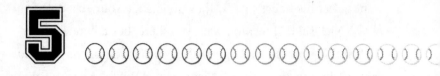

5

AT LAST IT WAS TIME FOR THE BLAZERS' FIRST GAME OF THE tournament, against the Rangers, one of the nine teams in their twelve-and-under division.

Last year, Nick's summer All-Star team had played as far away as White Plains in upstate New York. But this summer, because the Dream League was associated with the Yankees and Major League Baseball, all of the tournament games were scheduled to be played at Macombs Dam Park.

When it was the Blazers' turn to take batting practice, Coach Viera had Nick and Ben get their swings in first so that Nick would have ample time to warm up behind their bench on the first-base side of the field.

"I know you're geeked to get after it tonight," Ben said when he handed Nick the ball. "But you know our deal: we don't overthrow at the start."

Ben often used the word "we" when referring to Nick's pitching. They'd played for the first time together in the spring, but it felt as if they'd been a team their whole lives.

"The goal is to be throwing your best fastball in the last inning, not just the first," Ben reminded him.

"The way Verlander does," Nick said.

He was talking about Justin Verlander of the Astros. If Michael

Arroyo was Nick's all-time favorite power pitcher, Verlander was his favorite right-hander. The TV announcers were always marveling at how Verlander seemed to get stronger as the game went along, which was especially impressive given that he was in his mid-thirties.

"Wonder if Justin was as good as you when he was twelve," Ben said.

"Quit blowing smoke," Nick said, taking the ball from him.

"Dude," Ben said, "blowing smoke is your job, not mine." Nick rolled his eyes but couldn't help letting out a small laugh. If nothing else, it helped him relax.

The distance between the mound and home plate in Little League was forty-six feet. Ben carefully paced off fifteen yards, adding an extra foot at the end, before getting into his crouch. Nick began to warm up, soft-tossing at first, slowly dialing up his velocity, throwing loose and easy. And accurately tonight, much to his relief. You couldn't always tell how you'd pitch in a game just off a warm-up. But Nick felt good tonight from the start. Very good.

He finally signaled to Ben that he wanted to throw one last fastball. This time, he'd pretend he was facing the Rangers' leadoff man. Ben set his glove and didn't have to move it an inch as Nick delivered his final warm-up pitch. They both heard the sound the ball made. Ben liked to say that Nick's fastball was louder than the 4 train.

"All night long," Ben said as they walked over to the bench.

"All summer long."

Ben smiled. "K."

"You mean K like in 'strikeout'?" Nick said.

Ben reached out with his glove, and Nick tapped it with his own. "Pretty much."

Before the game started Coach Viera rounded up the Blazers and had them sit on the hill behind the field.

"I'm not one of those coaches who just tells you to have fun and try your hardest," he said, "even though I do want you to have fun and try your hardest. But you're allowed to want to win, too. Because those guys over there on the other team? You can bet they do."

He paced up and down in front of them.

"They keep score in sports for the same reason teachers give grades in school," Coach Viera said. "And I think what I'm looking at right now are a bunch of A students. But what I *think* doesn't matter. It's going to come down to how you boys play the game, starting right now."

He had their full attention. When he spoke to them about baseball, he always did. Nick's dad often said that people didn't just earn respect; they commanded it. Coach Viera was like that. It had been that way from their very first practice.

"About the fun part?" he said. "It was always my experience as a player that winning just makes everything a whole lot more fun."

He put out his hand now, and the Blazers got up and came down to where he was standing, moving in to put their hands on top of his.

"This isn't the longest season in the world," Coach said. "Let's see if we can make it one we'll all remember."

He looked around.

"Anybody else got anything they want to add?" he said.

Diego grinned. *This should be good,* Nick thought.

"I did," Diego said. "But then I *forgot* what I wanted to say about making this a tournament to *remember.*"

Everyone in the huddle had a good laugh.

"You're a funny guy, Diego," Coach said.

"Can't lie, Coach," Diego said. "I know."

At that, the Blazers broke the huddle and walked down the hill together to start their season. Because all the games were being played on the same field, the teams would alternate being home and visiting. Tonight, the Blazers were the home team. It didn't just mean they'd bat last. It meant Nick got to pitch first. Top of the first, top of the tournament. Fine with him.

Some parents and friends and people from the neighborhood watched the game from up on the hill. Many sat in the bleachers behind the Blazers' bench or behind first base. Others stood at the screen behind home plate, with the field out in front of them and the elevated subway tracks and apartment buildings in the distance. Nick had scrolled through hundreds of pictures of the old Yankee Stadium when it was on this side of the street, figuring out where it had stood before it was demolished and replaced by their fields. Derek Jeter, the great Yankees shortstop, believed there were baseball ghosts at the old Stadium. Not the kind that haunted and swooped overhead. But the memory of old players long gone. The ones who made the Yankees great, like Babe Ruth and Joe DiMaggio.

Sometimes Nick wondered if any of the ghosts still hung around here, or if they'd moved to the other side of 161st when Jeter and the Yankees did.

Maybe it didn't matter in the end.

Derek Jeter had his field of dreams on this side of the street, Nick told himself. *Now I have mine.*

Nick struck out the side in the top of the first.

When they got back to the bench, Ben told Nick that he'd thrown a total of twelve pitches. Just three more than the nine it would take to pitch an "immaculate inning": three batters, three strikeouts each. One of these days, Ben kept telling Nick, he'd get down to nine.

Tonight, he had been three over that limit in the first. There'd be plenty more opportunities in this game, and the season, to achieve it. The only batter who got to a two-ball count was the Rangers' number three hitter and center fielder, Lenny Rodriguez, a friend of Nick's from PS 359. Nick finally struck out Lenny, who had a sweet left-handed swing, on a two-and-two fastball at which Lenny swung so hard his helmet came flying off.

"Only one inning," Nick said, thinking about his pitch count.

"Yeah, but one that sure didn't stink," Ben said.

Diego tripled to lead off for the Blazers. One out later, Ben singled him home. The Blazers had the lead, that quickly. Nick was batting fifth. By then, the bases were loaded and Ben was on third, with one leg off the base, ready to sprint home. When Nick came up, he thought he'd hit one over Lenny's head. But Lenny, who could cover ground in the outfield almost as well as Diego, ran the ball down and made a great over-the-shoulder catch. Nick was almost to first when he did, and pointed out at Lenny in admiration.

Coach was right. Lenny wanted to win, too. They all did.

Ben took his chances, running all the way on Nick's hit. As soon as Lenny made the catch, he was off. By then, Lenny was too far out to make the throw home, and Ben crossed the plate for another run. He looped around toward the dugout, hurrying to get back into his catcher's gear. As he fastened the chest protector, he looked at Nick and said breathlessly, "Got enough runs?"

It had become an inside joke with them in the spring, even though Ben was only half kidding. As soon as their team was ahead by a single run, Ben wanted to know if Nick had enough runs to win the game.

Most of the time he did.

"Nice of you to knock in that last one for me," Nick said.

Ben grinned, strapping on the last bit of his gear. "I nicked them a little," he said. "Now you nick them a lot."

"I see what you did there," Nick said. "With my name, I mean."

"Diego's not the only funny one."

Nick gave a quick look over at the bleachers, and then to the hill behind the field. His parents hadn't arrived yet. Maybe his dad was delayed at the restaurant or had been asked to work a double shift. In a corner of Nick's mind, he knew there could be another reason his dad wasn't there. But he didn't want to go to a dark place like that. Not tonight. Anyway, Victor García always told his family that if the worst ever did happen, they'd hear it from him first.

Nick had his phone with him and knew his parents had Coach Viera's number. Ben's and Diego's, too. If there was any bad news, about his dad or his sister, it wouldn't take long for Nick to find out. There was an older woman in their building from Mexico,

Mrs. Gurriel, who checked in on Amelia when their parents were at work. Mrs. Gurriel was a retired nurse, so if there was an emergency, she'd know what to do . . .

Stop it, Nick told himself.

Amelia was fine. His parents were just late getting here from work. Simple as that.

Now you *get back to work.*

He struck out two more batters in the second and gave up his first hit, a bloop single that fell just in front of Diego's dive in short center. But Nick came right back and struck out the next guy on three pitches, then struck out two more in the top of the third, by which time the Blazers were ahead, 3–0.

As he came off the mound, Nick took another look over at the bleachers and exhaled. There, in their usual spot high up at the top, were his parents.

Seated between them was Amelia.

She didn't get to come to many of his games, especially during the summer when the sun didn't set until later in the evening. But this time she had gotten lucky. Or maybe Nick was the lucky one. There was some serious cloud cover in the South Bronx tonight. Not enough to make Nick worry about rain. Just enough to make it safe for Amelia to come outside and watch the game. She still wore a hat, but then, so did most people in the stands.

When she caught his eye, she smiled and waved. Nick smiled back and pointed to her, like she was his lucky charm.

He knew he wouldn't get to finish what he started in the first inning. Though he had a low pitch count so far, Nick figured

Coach Viera would take him out after the fifth. While eighty pitches was considered the maximum for twelve-year-old pitchers, Coach Viera thought that was too high and limited Nick's pitches to seventy.

"That's *my* magic number," Coach had said at their first practice.

"What if I've got a no-hitter going?" Nick had asked. "Or a perfect game?"

"If it ever comes to that, I *might* let you go to eighty," Coach said. "But no one game is more important than your arm. You know that, right?"

"You make my arm sound like something that ought to be in a museum," Nick said.

Coach winked and said, "Perhaps the one in Cooperstown, New York, someday."

That was where the National Baseball Hall of Fame was located.

Nick breezed through the fourth and fifth innings. After the fifth, as Nick suspected, Coach told him he was done for the night, clocking in at sixty-two pitches.

"Lot of baseball left to play," Coach Viera assured him, "even in this short season of ours."

Nick's final pitch of the night had produced his last strikeout, against the Rangers' shortstop, Jermaine Holmes, on an oh-and-two count. Nick didn't need to throw a strike to get him out. Based on the two wild swings Jermaine had already taken, he was likely going to get himself out no matter what Nick threw up there.

But Nick wanted to finish the night in style. He'd already accomplished everything he set out to against the Rangers by improving with each inning. His fastballs were on point; he could feel it. Ben felt it in his catcher's mitt, too.

His parents were here. Amelia was here. Nick was going to show them, and the rest of the crowd, how much arm he had left.

He came with high heat.

Jermaine had no chance. He swung under the pitch. Strike three. Nick's tenth strikeout of the game. The Blazers still led the Rangers 3–0 at the top of the sixth. Nick went to play second base, and their closer Kenny Locke, whom his teammates called "The Lock," pitched the last two innings, keeping the score frozen at 3–0.

And just like that, the Blazers were 1–0.

After the handshake line, and visiting with some friends on the Rangers, Nick and his family started for home. They chatted about the game the whole way, though Nick let his family do most of the talking. By now, they knew Nick didn't much like talking about himself. It was just as well, since tomorrow he and Ben would likely rehash his five innings on the mound, pitch by pitch. Ben had the kind of memory that let him replay whole parts of the game inside his head. But that was for tomorrow. For now, Nick was just content to have his family around him, feeling as if he were floating home. It wasn't just the Rangers who couldn't touch him tonight.

For right now, on Opening Night of the tournament, Nick actually felt as if no one could.

Not all of Nick's problems were big ones.

He wasn't even sure one of them could be considered a problem. It was a happy one, if there was such a thing. Or maybe it was just that: a thing. One involving a girl. He'd first met her in the fifth grade, when her family moved to the Bronx from Brooklyn.

Marisol Pérez.

She was the first girl Nick had ever liked. Or "*like*-liked," as Diego put it. Nick usually told Diego to shut it whenever he mentioned Marisol. But he knew Diego was right. He did *like*-like her. Not only that; he wanted her to *like*-like him back. He thought about it a lot, and way more than he wanted to.

Whatever space in Nick's brain wasn't occupied by baseball or his family was reserved for Marisol, not that he'd admit that to anyone but himself.

"Are you thinking about baseball or girls?" Diego would sometimes ask out of the blue.

"Baseball," Nick would always say.

Though what he really wanted to say was *both*.

He was hoping Marisol might come to the game last night, even though she was always finding ways to tell him—and not in a mean way—that she didn't care all that much for baseball. Of course, Marisol knew about Nick's gift for pitching. But baseball wasn't her sport. Tennis was, and she had her own dreams of going pro someday—"the Serena Williams of the South Bronx" was how she put it.

"Just because you love tennis doesn't mean you have to hate baseball," Nick said to her now.

They were sitting on the front stoop of her building, two down from Nick's, on the same side of the street. Ladies' voices traveled through an open window above them, and Nick and Marisol watched as a few neighborhood kids biked past on the sidewalk.

"You know I don't *hate* baseball. I'm just never going to love it," she admitted.

"You don't have to love it," Nick said. "I just feel like you're never even going to like it."

"Well, no," she said. "But in tennis, the action really only stops at the end of a set or when the players change sides. In baseball, the action is *always* stopping. Come on. Even *you* have to admit there's more lag time than actual play time."

"Not true," Nick said. "If you ever come to one of my games, you'll see how many guys are in motion once the ball is in play. Everybody has somewhere to go."

Marisol smiled. She clearly enjoyed teasing him this way. It was hardly the first time they'd had this kind of back-and-forth about baseball and tennis (and it wouldn't be the last). It was as if they were rallying across the net at each other, which, if Nick was being honest, was the closest he'd ever come to actually playing tennis.

"But wait," she said, spotting an opening in his argument. "I thought the object of the game for a strikeout pitcher was to *avoid* having the ball in play. That's what you're always saying, isn't it? That you want to strike out the whole world?"

Nick saw an opening of his own.

"Right. But that's how our two sports are alike. I'm always wanting to put the ball past my opponent," he said, "and so are you. And when you finally do, that's when *you* sit down."

He smiled now, satisfied with his response. What could she possibly say back?

"But I don't get to sit as long as you do between innings," she said, smirking. "Or when you're waiting to bat."

Nick hung his head between his legs. "Am I ever going to win this argument?"

"It's not an argument!" she said, nudging his shoulder so he'd lift his head to face her. "It's just a game the two of us like to play."

"Who says I like it?"

"What," she said, "you don't like being with me?"

Now Nick's smile disappeared and he could feel a flush rising in his cheeks, something that happened a lot when he was with Marisol. Unfortunately, there was no way of stopping it.

"You know better than that," he said.

"Yeah, I do," she said. "Just wanted to see you sweat."

He did like being with her. A lot. And it wasn't just because of her familiar smile, or flowing auburn hair, or deep brown eyes with flecks of gold. He genuinely felt comfortable when he was around her. He liked being with her now, sitting on this stoop, watching the street traffic and listening to the Latin pop music playing from somewhere above them. Marisol sang along with the melody. Her parents were from Puerto Rico, and she was fluent in both English and Spanish. Nick knew a little Spanish, but not enough to carry out an entire conversation. Not like Marisol. Perched next to her on the stoop, he realized he liked hanging out with her in a different way—*way* different—than he liked being with Ben and Diego.

Despite all the teasing and fake arguments, Nick understood that she wasn't making fun of him.

She just loved having fun *with* him.

"All I'm saying is if you watched more baseball, you'd appreciate it more," Nick said, making his point. "Maybe you could start by catching one of my games in the tournament . . ."

"How do you know I wasn't watching last night?" she said.

A breath caught in Nick's throat.

"You were?" he said, not even caring how excited he sounded that she might have been there, seeing him pitch against the Rangers.

"I *might* have walked over with my dad to see the first two innings," she said.

"Why didn't you let me know?"

"I didn't want to put any more pressure on you," she said. "Or make you try to show off."

"I never show off," he said, a little hurt Marisol would think that.

"I know," she said. "Just messing with you."

She stood up.

"Let's walk," she said.

"Where?"

"Do you care?"

Nick did not.

So they walked south down Grand Concourse, took a right at 161st Street, and made their way down the hill in the direction of Yankee Stadium.

When Nick was lucky enough to go to Yankee games with his dad, he loved taking this walk from their building, surrounded by crowds of people flowing like a river down to the ballpark. They filtered in through Babe Ruth Plaza on 161st, walking up the steps and through the turnstiles into the great baseball place.

There was no Yankee game today, no hordes of fans on the sidewalk, just the normal buzz of the city spread out around them, and the familiar roar of the trains pulling in and out of the station above them.

But when they passed underneath the subway tracks, to their surprise, they did spot a crowd at Babe Ruth Plaza. Once they got closer, they could see a satellite truck with two TV station cameras set up at the top of the stairs.

Nick and Marisol made their way through the masses, until they could see what the cameras were pointed at.

Nick couldn't believe his eyes. It was Michael Arroyo. Here. In the flesh. Nick's heart started pounding. At the same time his breathing became short and quick, and his legs seemed to stop working, forcing him to stop cold. But Marisol, who seemed to have no shyness in her at all, took him by the arm and got him moving again. Together, they pressed through closer and closer to Nick's hero. Marisol asked a taller man in the crowd what was happening.

"TV commercial," he said.

"For what?" Marisol asked.

"Some RBI program run by Major League Baseball," the man replied.

"My friend," Marisol said, nodding her head at Nick, "is a part of that program." She turned to Nick, but he stood frozen, staring at Michael, mere feet from where he stood.

"That's great, kid," the man said. "But the only kind of RBI I care about are ones for the Yankees."

Marisol still had Nick's arm in her grip, pulling him to the front of the crowd while doing her best not to shove anybody in the process. Marisol was good like that.

When they reached the front, they could see Michael wearing his home Yankees jersey, the white one with the famous blue pinstripes. Nick didn't have to see it to know it had the number 34 on the back. The same number El Grande had worn.

"I can't believe I'm this close to him," Nick whispered, finally finding his voice again.

"It's why we had to get to the front," Marisol whispered back. "Who knows when you might get this chance again?"

He'd never discussed the MVP award with Marisol. Never told her about the chance he might earn to throw out the first pitch at Yankee Stadium. So she didn't know there was a possibility he could be this close to Michael again.

"I wish I had a ball with me," Nick said with a note of regret. "Maybe I could've gotten him to sign it when he's done."

"You don't need an autograph," she said, as if she were stating an absolute fact.

"I don't?"

"For today," she said, "just be happy you're breathing the same air as a legend."

Nick closed his eyes and inhaled deeply. They watched as Michael read off cue cards that a woman behind the camera held for him, until finally the camera lights turned off and they heard a man in a headset say, "That's a wrap." At that, the crowd descended on Michael, holding out baseballs or slips of paper for autographs and shouting his name to get his attention.

Nick didn't add his voice to the clamor. He wasn't sure he could have, even if he wanted to. Just standing there in front of Yankee Stadium, watching Michael Arroyo wave and smile at his fans, was enough.

A woman who must have worked for the Yankees came over and announced that, unfortunately, Michael wouldn't have time to sign any autographs today, as he was already late for a luncheon appearance in Manhattan. So Michael gave one final wave before turning away, and then he was gone.

The crowd began to disperse, but Nick stayed behind a few extra minutes. Finally, Marisol told him that Michael wasn't coming back and it was time for them to head home.

"That was coo," she said.

It was her way of saying "cool."

"Seriously," Nick said. "That really is the closest I've ever been to him. The one time I saw him pitch in person, my dad and I sat way up in the bleachers."

From everything Nick had read about the Yankees and Michael Arroyo, he knew at the old Yankee Stadium, the players' parking lot was out in the open, so kids could line up and watch the Yankees walk past on their way inside. It wasn't that way anymore. Now the players drove their cars inside a parking garage beneath the new Stadium. If you waited, all you could see were cars going past before disappearing underground.

"That can be you in a couple of years," Marisol said. It was scary how she could read Nick's mind. He'd just been thinking the same thing.

But as much as she knew, there was still so much she didn't.

And he didn't want her to.

"When does he pitch here again?" she asked, swinging her hand dangerously close to his.

"Saturday," Nick said, inwardly debating whether or not to grab it.

Then he was quiet, and so was she. He liked that about Marisol: she wasn't afraid of silence, and therefore, it was never awkward between the two of them. In fact, it relieved some of the pressure on Nick, since there was a part of him that always worried he might say something stupid in front of her.

And he wanted to look bad in front of Marisol about as much as he wanted to look bad on the baseball field.

So he never told her about the issues his family faced. Marisol's parents were born in America, and it wasn't like she'd ever ask whether Nick's were, too. It never came up in conversation, either, so he wasn't necessarily lying to her. It just felt like too much. Having to explain how every day was spent looking over his shoulder for Official People working for the government, for ICE, for the police. The agony of worrying about whether his parents would be able to remain in the country long enough for Amelia to turn twenty-one, when she could sponsor them for green cards.

He never told Marisol about how he feared the police as much as he feared ICE, and for good reason.

Marisol's father was a New York City policeman.

7

NICK'S FATHER HAD RAISED NICK AND AMELIA TO RESPECT THE LAW, even though they both knew he'd broken it once.

When Nick was eight and Amelia was nine, Victor deemed them old enough to hear about the biggest mistake of his life. He sat them down on the living room sofa to share his story.

"At the time, I thought I was breaking the law for a good reason," he said. "But in the end, it didn't matter. I still broke it."

Nick's parents were already married when they came to the Bronx on tourist visas. For a time, they lived with one of Graciela's cousins in a tiny apartment on Jerome Avenue, not so far from where they lived now. Victor García first found work as a dishwasher in a diner in Spanish Harlem. Graciela's cousin set her up with babysitting jobs in the neighborhood.

But they wanted better jobs and their own apartment, promising themselves they wouldn't even think of starting a family until they had both. Victor had grown up working in his uncle's restaurant in Santo Domingo, the capital of the Dominican Republic. His big dream was to become a chef in a New York City restaurant, and maybe someday open up a restaurant of his own.

So he applied for waiter jobs whenever there were new listings. Finally, a friend of his who worked at a restaurant in Upper Manhattan told him about an opening for a waiter position. He was able to get Victor an interview the following morning.

Nick's dad and mom had so little money, yet they insisted on paying rent for the small room they stayed in at Graciela's cousin's. After that, there was barely enough for them to get by. Nick's dad told him and Amelia that sometimes the only things in his pocket were a MetroCard, which enabled you to ride the subway, and a few dollars.

On the morning of his interview, Victor got to the 161st Street station and discovered that his monthly MetroCard had expired. Though he'd made sure to leave the apartment with plenty of time to get to his interview, he'd also left without any money in his wallet. He'd planned to pick up his paycheck at the diner on his way home.

That didn't help him when he got to the subway turnstiles.

He knew he had to get downtown for the interview, and couldn't be late. This was his shot at a good, well-paying job. They might not become citizens right away, but having stable jobs, getting their own apartment, and settling down—these were all ways of making America feel like home.

Victor felt as though he didn't have a choice. It'd be foolish to pass up an opportunity like this. So after taking a quick glance around for onlookers, he jumped the turnstile, promising to himself, and maybe to God, that he'd find a way to right the wrong. Offer someone a free swipe on his MetroCard, perhaps. Someone who found himself in similar circumstances.

But Victor never got that chance. Because despite his

precautions, someone *had* been paying attention: a New York City transit officer.

The man arrested Victor García on the spot, and he was taken to the 44th Precinct on 169th Street. There, he was fingerprinted and spent most of the next twenty-four hours in jail, before appearing in court the next day for an arraignment, where he was formally charged for his crime. He was appointed a lawyer by the court, a public defender who stood next to Victor García in the courtroom as the judge assigned another court date, three weeks later. The lawyer explained to Victor that the worst they'd do was fine him a penalty charge.

When Victor asked how much, the lawyer said it might be as much as five hundred dollars.

At the time, it may as well have been five million.

"But you're going into the system," the policeman said.

"What kind of system?"

"The kind for people who have a criminal record."

It scared him as much as the amount of the fine. And because there was no way Victor would ever be able to pay it, he didn't show up for his court date.

New York City later stopped prosecuting most people for fare-jumping, simply because it was clogging up the city's court system, which had far more important things to handle. But that did nothing to help Victor García now. He *was* in the system, and because he hadn't shown up in court, there was an outstanding warrant out for his arrest. To top it all off, his tourist visa had also expired.

"But you were only trying to get a job," Amelia had said.

"And you said the laws have changed now," an eight-year-old Nick piped up.

"They have," Victor told them. "But so, too, has the attitude toward immigrants in this country. Now if I am ever arrested for anything again, they have my fingerprints in the system, and that's all they'd need to take action."

Nick peered over at Amelia across the couch. She sat completely still, her back straight, an expression of concern settled over her face. As the younger brother, Nick usually took his cues from Amelia, so he could tell this was far more serious than he initially thought.

"Now, I don't tell you this to scare you or make you worry," Victor said. "Everything's fine, and your mom and I are good, hardworking people. I've learned my lesson, and if I could go back in time and decide not to jump that turnstile, I would. But moving on, there's nothing I would do to put the two of you in danger, me entienden?" Victor took Nick's and Amelia's hands in his.

Nick and Amelia nodded solemnly, but on the inside, Nick's chest tightened and his heart pounded wildly. If his father made one more mistake, it could put the entire family in jeopardy. Because if Victor and Graciela were sent back to the DR, they'd take Nick and Amelia with them.

Nick knew enough about baseball to know how many major-league ballplayers had come from the Dominican Republic to the United States.

He didn't want to be one going the other way.

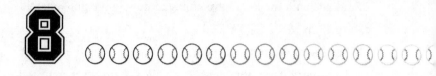

THE BLAZERS WON THEIR NEXT GAME, AGAINST THE STARS, improving their record to 2–0. Their third game, and Nick's next start, was scheduled for the following Tuesday night against the Bronx Giants.

Not only would Nick be pitching again, but so would the Giants' ace, Eric Dobbs. He was tall, left-handed, and one of the strongest pitchers in the league. Nick knew how good he was from pitching against him in the spring. Eric knew how good he was, too, and wasn't shy about letting everybody know it.

"You know what they say about guys being born on third base and thinking they hit a triple?" Diego said. "Eric thinks he's better than everyone because his dad works for the Yankees."

It was true. Eric's dad did work in the scouting department for the Yankees, which everyone knew because Eric never shut up about it.

Every game in the Dream League tournament felt big because there were so few of them to begin with. But this one felt bigger to Nick, and he knew why. Eric was the opposing starter, and he had his eyes on the same two prizes as Nick: winning the championship and winning the MVP award.

They didn't have a practice scheduled for the day before the Giants game. But as far as Nick, Ben, and Diego were concerned, every summer day was supposed to have some baseball in it somewhere. No one was using their field at Macombs Dam Park on Monday morning, so for now, it belonged to them.

The fields at Macombs Dam Park weren't the nicest they'd ever seen. They had all played on better fields when they traveled in their All-Star league last summer. But the kids who played on those fields didn't have Yankee Stadium in their backyard. So Nick, Ben, and Diego never felt cheated growing up in the Bronx. The city worked hard to make this new version of the park even bigger and better than the original across the street. This was prime baseball real estate, in close proximity to the home field of the greatest major-league team in the country. What was the phrase? Location, location, location.

They brought bats, gloves, and some old baseballs to toss around. When it was just the three of them like this, they invented their own hitting and fielding games to try out.

Nick wasn't allowed to pitch on days before his starts. So Ben pitched, and Diego took a few turns as well. As good of a catcher as Ben was, he could have been a star pitcher himself; his arm was that true and strong. But Ben had his own baseball dreams of being a catcher in the big leagues someday. Every time Nick urged him to try pitching, Ben's response was that he was planning to stay behind the plate until somebody better came along.

So far, no one had.

After they'd had enough of hitting, Nick jogged over to second base and Ben went to first, while Diego hit them ground balls. After a while, Diego said he wanted to pitch a pretend inning with Ben catching and Nick acting as the home-plate ump calling balls and strikes.

After Nick called his first pitch a ball, Diego threw his arms up in mock anger and moaned, "You're squeezing me, ump!"

Then Nick said something he'd heard an umpire say once: "When it's a strike, son, you'll be the first to know."

"Man, throwing strikes is *hard*," Diego said, "even when there's no batter."

Ben grinned and jerked a thumb in Nick's direction. "Not for him."

An hour or so later, they took their stuff up the hill and sat down with their water bottles, watching the rest of the day go by in their corner of the Bronx.

"I wish the game with the Giants was starting right now," Diego said, squinting up at the sun.

"Careful what you wish for," said Ben. "The guys we're facing tomorrow night do *not* stink."

"Are you kidding? Eric's one of the best pitchers in the tournament," Nick said.

"But not *the* best," Diego was quick to interject.

Nick sighed. "I guess we'll find out tomorrow night."

"You can go ahead and guess," Ben said. "But Diego and me? We already *know*."

Nick hoped they were right, but didn't want to believe it too hard. After all, he wasn't the only one in the Dream League with a chance to win the MVP this season. Ben and Diego were just as capable as he was, and there were plenty of talented players all over the league. But in Nick's brain, Eric Dobbs was his biggest competition by far. Without having to know Eric all that well, Nick was keenly aware of how much Eric wanted that MVP trophy. Knowing that Eric's father worked for the Yankees, Nick could imagine how special throwing out the first pitch would be for him.

"Hey," Ben said, waving a hand in front of Nick's face. "Where'd you just go?"

"I'm right here," Nick said.

"No, you had that faraway look," Diego said.

"What?" Nick said.

"You know—the one where you've gone off to visit the planet Nick," Diego said.

"You think he was alone on that trip?" Ben asked Diego with a sly look in his eye.

"Hold up," Diego said, mouth agape. "You think there might have been a . . . *girl* on the trip with him?"

"Here we go," Nick said, knowing there was nothing he could do to stop this runaway train.

"You think they play tennis on the planet Nick?" Diego said. He could hardly hold in his laughter.

Ben was already rolling in the grass, cackling.

"You just crack yourself up, don't you?" Nick said to Diego.

"Not just myself, from the looks of it," Diego said, gesturing to Ben.

"But did you notice *I* wasn't laughing?"

Ben gave him a shove. "You never think it's funny when we talk about Marisol."

Diego feigned surprise. "I didn't mention any names. Were we talking about *Marisol*?"

Nick felt himself blush at the sound of her name, and instantly regretted it.

"The girl who I heard might be coming to watch you pitch tomorrow night?" Ben said.

Nick whipped his head around toward Ben. "How do you know that?" So much for saving face. "Is she really coming? Or are you messing with me?"

"Her brother *may* have mentioned she had plans to stop by," Ben said, clearly enjoying this torture session.

Diego grinned. "Did the game just get bigger for you?"

"It's big enough already," Nick said, because it was.

They decided to get in a few more swings before breaking for the afternoon. Then the three of them headed toward Ben's building and spent the rest of the evening in his apartment watching one of their favorite old baseball movies, *The Sandlot*. They'd seen it about a thousand times apiece, and practically knew it by heart. But they loved how the star of the team, Benny "the Jet" Rodriguez, ended up making it to the big leagues, with his best pal, Scotty Smalls, growing up to be a professional sports announcer.

It was a good baseball movie to end a good baseball day.

Unfortunately, that very same night, Nick's parents had to take Amelia to the hospital.

IT WAS A CLINIC, ACTUALLY: THE EINSTEIN COMMUNITY HEALTH Outreach Free Clinic on Walton Avenue, called ECHO by the people in the neighborhood. The clinic took in patients who couldn't afford costly health insurance or hospital stays. It was why the free clinic, Nick's mom said, was one of the blessings of their lives.

"Someday we will have the best health insurance money can buy," Graciela García had once said to Nick. "But for now you have to be like your father and me."

"I always try to be like you and Dad," Nick said.

His mom had kissed him on the cheek and said, "I meant that for now you must remain healthy, mi hijo. La salud es la mayor riqueza." She was right. His health *was* the most valuable thing, and Nick couldn't argue with that.

Amelia hadn't fainted this time, something that'd happened to her on several occasions. But tonight, she started to feel light-headed while watching TV, and was experiencing shortness of breath. In the past, she had just waited for the symptoms to pass.

But this time the symptoms didn't pass. It was only about a fifteen-minute walk to the free clinic, but walking wasn't an option. So Graciela called Mrs. Gurriel, whose nephew was an

Uber driver. He'd just dropped someone on River Avenue, and agreed to come straight to 164th Street. As always, Mrs. Gurriel said her nephew would accept no payment.

"I keep telling you, we're not a charity case," Nick's mom said to Mrs. Gurriel in front of their building, after helping Amelia into the back seat of the car. "My husband and I both have jobs."

"Think of this as a family rate," Mrs. Gurriel said, winking. "Now go."

Mrs. Gurriel sat upstairs with Nick after his mom left with Amelia. Victor, who was just finishing his shift at the restaurant, said he would meet them at the clinic. It was usually a short visit for Amelia after having one of the doctors examine her. But if the clinic was crowded, his sister would be there longer. So far, she'd never had to stay the night.

As a former nurse, Mrs. Gurriel had seen plenty of cases of lupus, and assured Nick that Amelia's was a milder version than most. But that didn't do much to ease Nick's concerns.

"Is she ever going to be normal?" he said.

They were sitting in his living room with the Yankee game on in the background. Nick was barely watching it, though he caught Mrs. Gurriel sneaking looks at the screen.

"What am I always telling you?" Mrs. Gurriel said. "Your sister isn't normal, and neither are you."

She was tall and thin, with a full head of pearly white hair tucked into a bun at the nape of her neck.

"But I *want* us to be normal!" Nick said, a bit impatiently. "I want *everything* to be normal."

"When I say that you and your sister aren't normal," Mrs.

Gurriel said, "I don't mean it in a bad way. It's my way of telling you that you are both destined for great things."

"You always sound so sure of that," Nick said, not altogether certain why he was so angry to hear her say it.

"It's because I can see the future," she said, and that frustrated Nick even more. He didn't believe anyone could predict the future—at least not accurately—but he decided to humor Mrs. Gurriel anyway.

"Okay, so when you see our future," Nick said, "do you see all of us living safely in America?"

"I do."

"How can you be so sure?"

"Because that is the way your family's story is supposed to end," she said.

"But when do we get the happy ending?" Nick persisted.

"I can't see *everything*," she said. "When I was a little girl in Mexico, my mother used to read me a poem. It was about doing the right things to get into heaven, so that one day God could answer all our questions about why things in our life happened the way they did."

"I have a question for you, Mrs. G," Nick said. "Do you think Amelia is okay right now?"

She nodded without hesitation.

"Another vision?"

Mrs. G laughed. "No," she said, "just my training as a nurse."

Amelia returned home not long after the Yankees won their game. The doctor gave her some medicine to help her breathing, but it also caused drowsiness, so a half hour later, she was fast asleep.

Nick had just finished brushing his teeth when he came out of the bathroom and heard his parents talking in the kitchen. They were trying to keep their voices down, but if Nick stood behind the wall in the hallway, he could hear them faintly.

"I'm glad you called me," Victor García said.

"I didn't think it was serious this time," Nick's mom said. "But I know you hate it when I *don't* call."

"Knowing is always better than not knowing," he said matter-of-factly.

"It's just that you have so much else on your mind."

"And you don't?"

Then there was a pocket of silence, until Nick heard something he didn't often hear.

The sound of his mother crying. It was like a punch to the gut.

He wanted to comfort her. Tell her everything was going to be all right for their family, even if he didn't believe it himself.

Instead he walked softly across the hall to his sister's room. At least she was home, in her own bed. At least for tonight she was better. That was enough for him.

Amelia's face was illuminated only by the streetlights outside her window. She snored lightly, even though she'd deny it if Nick ever brought it up.

But there was a half smile on her face. Nick wondered if she was healthy in her dreams, if she was able to go outside whenever she wanted. Sometimes he'd write stories about her transforming into a bird, flying across New York City, free from illness and fear and limitation.

As he stepped out of the room and tried to shut her door

without waking her, Nick heard her say, "Don't worry about me."

"There's no possible way you're awake right now. I can hear you snoring."

"Liar."

Nick threw his hands up in defense. "All I'm saying is, I heard what I heard."

"Well, obviously you can't hear very well, because then you'd know how loud you were stomping around my room," she said.

Nick gasped for effect, and Amelia giggled under her blanket.

"Night, sis," he said.

"Night."

10

THE BLAZERS' GAME AGAINST THE GIANTS WAS SCHEDULED FOR SIX o'clock Tuesday night. Nick, Ben, and Diego were at the field promptly at four thirty.

"No lie—if I stayed home one minute longer, I was going to lose my mind," Diego said.

"Didn't that happen a long time ago?" Ben said.

Diego turned and looked at Nick. "Aren't you going to defend me?"

"From the truth?" Nick asked, slapping Ben five above Diego's head.

Of the three, Diego *was* the funniest. Nick and Ben could hold their own, but Diego's humor just came naturally. Ben was the quietest and most introspective of the group. He said he got that from his dad, who'd told him it was best to talk only when you had something to say.

Nick wasn't quite as loud as Diego, or as shy as Ben. He was somewhere in the middle, but that was why they made such a good team.

A team within a team now, with the rest of the Blazers at Macombs Dam Park. The Giants players were now trickling onto the field to warm up.

"We could end up playing these guys in the championship," Diego said.

"I'd sign up for that right now," said Ben.

"Let's just win the game tonight," Nick said, "and worry about later later."

Diego snorted. "Later *later*?" Then to Ben, "And this kid calls himself a writer?"

It was common knowledge that Nick's favorite activity, other than baseball, was writing. He was the only one of his friends who actually enjoyed the assignments from their English teacher.

"You know what I meant," Nick said, elbowing Diego in the ribs.

"Hate to interrupt this precious moment," said Ben, "but are we ready to do this?"

"You don't have to ask me twice," Nick said.

Ben reached down and pulled Nick to his feet. Then Nick grabbed Diego and they set off down the hill toward the field.

11

THE BLAZERS WERE DESIGNATED AS THE VISITING TEAM TONIGHT, which meant they batted first.

It also meant Eric Dobbs got to pitch first.

"Eric say anything to you when he got here?" Ben asked Nick.

They were seated on the Blazers' bench, on the third-base side of the field tonight, watching Eric take the mound to begin his warm-up pitches.

"Nah," Nick said. "But it's not like we've ever been boys."

"Knowing him," Diego said, "I doubt he feels that way about any of his own teammates."

"Guy does have filthy stuff, though," Nick said, sounding almost jealous.

"Not filthier than yours," Ben was quick to say.

"Seriously, though? I can't treat this like a game of one-on-one with Eric," Nick said.

That made Diego laugh.

"Yeah," he said to Nick, "keep telling yourself that."

Coach Viera waved the rest of the Blazers over to the bench and knelt in front of them in the grass.

"I'm gonna get right to it," he said. "We all know who we're playing. And we know how good their pitcher is. But here's what *I* know. Our pitcher is better, and our best game blows theirs out of the water. Now we just have to go out there and play it."

Diego was leading off. Andy Friedman, the Blazers' shortstop, was batting second. Ben was third. Their first baseman, Darryl Taylor, was at cleanup. Nick was batting fifth.

Nick studied Eric as Diego stepped into the batter's box. Unbelievably, he looked even taller than he had in the spring, but was still just as skinny, with wisps of blond hair coming out the back of his cap.

Nick also noticed that Eric's glove looked brand new. Even from the bench, he could tell it was the new Michael Arroyo model, black with blue trim. Nick looked down at his own, older Arroyo glove, and couldn't help feeling envious. But then he quickly shook his head, as if trying to shake the thought out.

You don't pitch with your glove, he told himself.

Diego was ready to hit, having taken a few practice swings before settling into his stance behind the plate. Eric, though, wasn't quite ready to pitch. He made Diego wait, rubbing up the ball, taking one last breath as he turned to his fielders, like he was checking inventory.

When he was finally ready, he turned back around, set himself on the rubber, and blew a fastball past Diego for strike one. Diego could generally catch up with anyone's fastball, including Nick's. But he hadn't come close to Eric's. He swung and missed for strikes two and three, before handing off the bat to Andy and kicking up dirt on his way back to the Blazers' bench. His back was turned, so Diego didn't see Eric Dobbs staring him down longer than necessary. Longer than Nick thought the moment afforded for simply getting the first out of a game.

Ben saw what Nick saw.

"Game on," he whispered into Nick's ear, before walking over to the on-deck circle.

Eric struck out Andy Friedman on three pitches for the second out of the top of the first. Six pitches, six strikes. Maybe Eric was the one on his way to an immaculate inning.

Now it was Ben's turn to face Eric.

Eric was working fast and efficient. Ben had it in mind to change that. Ben Kelly was usually old-school as a ballplayer. He didn't even wear batting gloves. But he took his time stepping into the box, wiping some dirt on his hands, rubbing it onto the handle of the bat.

Nick felt himself smiling, and his teammates chuckled next to him, enjoying this little act. Ben was slowing down the pace of play to a crawl, as Eric fidgeted on the mound, ready to throw.

When Ben did step in, he stood closer to the plate than usual. Nick knew what he was doing: trying to take the inside of home plate away from Eric. Eric threw a fastball that probably caught the inside corner. Ben jumped back, raising his arms.

The home-plate umpire called it a ball.

"Don't let him beg that call!" Eric boomed, staring in at the ump.

The ump didn't hesitate. He stepped around the Giants' catcher and Ben, right in front of the plate.

"What did you say, son?" he said.

"That was a strike," Eric said, not backing down, his voice as loud as before.

"Here's all the ways a strike is a strike, just so we're clear," the ump said, ticking off each one on his fingers. "When the batter swings and misses. When he fouls one off. Or when I say it's a strike."

Maybe all home-plate umps say this at one point or another, Nick thought.

"Just so we're clear on something else?" the ump said, and Eric lowered his head. "You pitch. I'll call balls and strikes. That way we don't have to have this conversation again."

Eric came back inside with his next pitch. Nick was almost positive he would. But Ben was ready, covering the inside of the plate with his quick bat, and lining a ball over the head of the Giants' third baseman.

Unfortunately, Darryl popped out to end the inning.

Nick's turn to pitch now.

He sat on the bench while Ben changed into his catcher's gear.

"Just because Eric came out hot doesn't mean we have to," Ben said.

"Got it," said Nick.

"We just pitch our game."

Nick nodded to confirm.

Ben jogged out and took his position. Nick loosened up and threw his warm-up pitches. Before the Giants' leadoff man stepped in, Nick took a scan of the bleachers. His dad had said he'd probably be late to the game after work. Nick's mom was staying home with Amelia, who was feeling better, but not well enough to come out.

It was just Nick and baseball for now. Ball in his hand, Ben's mitt as a target, and a game he really, *really* wanted to win.

Control what you can control.

Behind the field Nick glimpsed cars beginning to file out of parking garages and lots near Yankee Stadium. The Yankee game was set to begin in about forty-five minutes.

But as the Giants' catcher, José Barrea, took his stance, Nick's focus came right back to the mound he stood on. Oh, Nick was aware of the chatter from his infielders behind him. But after years of getting accustomed to the constant buzz on the field, he was able to block out the noise and just pitch when it was time to pitch.

He didn't throw his best fastball to José, but he didn't have to. José swung underneath the ball for strike one. He took a called strike, fouled a ball off, swung and missed badly for strike three. Then Nick struck out Carlo Rotella, the Giants' shortstop. Carlo took a called third strike and didn't complain. It was a perfect pitch. On the outside corner. At the knees. Unhittable.

Eric Dobbs came to the plate. He batted left-handed, same as he threw, and Nick remembered from the spring that he had home-run power, pretty much to all fields. So as much as Nick wanted to strike him out, he reminded himself that the object was to just *get* him out.

Ben called for a changeup, knowing everybody on the field was expecting Nick to challenge him right away. But Eric wasn't fooled, and ripped a screamer of a line drive just foul past first base.

Okay, Nick thought, *scratch the changeup.*

He threw a fastball high for a ball. One-and-one. He came inside next, and got the call on the corner that Eric had failed to get against Ben. Nick saw Eric turn toward the ump, as if he wanted to say something, but he was smart enough not to this time.

Ben set up his mitt on the outside corner. Didn't have to move it an inch as Eric swung and missed for strike three. As Nick walked off the mound, he took a quick look back, to see Eric in the batter's box, following Nick with his eyes and nodding in his direction.

"What was that all about?" Ben asked when they were back at the bench.

"Eric being Eric," Nick said with a shrug.

"You better stay loose when you get up there," Ben said, knowing Nick was leading off for the Blazers in the top of the second.

"Why?"

"Just in case Eric puts you on your butt."

"Why would he do that?"

"Oh, I don't know . . . Eric being Eric?" Ben said.

Eric put Nick on the ground with his first pitch.

It wasn't a flagrant knockdown pitch. It didn't come anywhere close to Nick's head. But it was far enough inside that Nick had to jump back from the plate. As he did, his spikes caught in the dirt and he went down.

"If it wasn't a hardball sport," Nick's dad once told him, "they wouldn't make everybody wear helmets."

Nick didn't even look at Eric. He didn't want to give him the satisfaction. Instead, he picked himself up and got back into the box. Having gotten Nick's attention by coming inside, Eric tried to go away with the next pitch. But Nick was on it, taking it to right field, getting enough bat on the ball that it rolled between the right fielder and center fielder. He ended up with a double.

Sometimes after he'd get a clean hit like that, he'd give a quick clap of his hands once he got to his base. Not this time. He just turned and stared over at Ben and Diego on the bench. They both pointed at him. Ronnie Lester, who was playing second tonight, singled to center. Nick scored easily: 1–0, Blazers.

As soon as he sat down between Ben and Diego, Nick knew what was coming.

"Got enough of a lead?" Ben said, grinning.

"Can't believe you even had to ask," Nick said, taking a slug of his water bottle.

Eric settled down after that, pitching like a complete star. But so did Nick. Through the fourth inning, it seemed as though they were determined to match each other strikeout for strikeout. Nick wasn't so off the mark when he predicted he and Eric would face off in a game of one-on-one.

But it remained 1–0 for the Blazers.

Nick's pitch count was low enough that after the bottom of the fourth, Coach Viera said he might allow Nick to pitch into the sixth inning tonight.

"What about going the distance?" Nick said.

Coach grinned. "Give a mouse a cookie . . ."

"And this mouse wants the whole cake," Nick replied.

"One pitch at a time, one hitter at a time, one inning at a time," Coach said.

"Control what you can control, right, Coach?"

"Hey," Coach said, putting out his hand for a low five. "That's my line."

Nick struck out the side in the bottom of the fifth. When he got back to the bench, he said to Coach, "One more?"

Coach agreed. "One more."

Nick punched a fist into his glove in triumph.

"We having any fun yet?" Coach said.

Nick grinned. "More fun if we get a couple of insurance runs to put this thing away."

"Tell the guys that if they do, and we close this baby out, I'm taking everybody for ice cream."

"Is that a bribe?" Nick said.

"You could say that." Then Coach ran out to the third-base coaching box.

Eric was still out there for the Giants. Diego finally got a hit off him, his first of the night, a clean single to left. Andy bunted him to second. Ben singled Diego home. The score was 2–0. Eric was getting tired, and it showed. But he had enough left to strike out Darryl, and get Nick on a hard line drive to the shortstop.

The Blazers had only gotten one insurance run. It still felt like a lot to Nick against a team like the Giants. Eric might be tiring, but Nick wasn't. He only took a few warm-up pitches and signaled to Ben that he was good to go. He glanced over to his right, at Yankee Stadium, the lights ringing the top of the great baseball place, the roar of the fans, the music pumping, and the voice of the public address announcer echoing into Macombs Dam Park.

Nick had been so locked into the game that he hadn't looked over at the bleachers for a while. When he did now, he saw Victor García sitting high in the corner, still dressed in the white button-down shirt and black pants he wore at the restaurant.

Nick's eyes wandered up and surprise registered on his face. Right behind his dad, in the last row, sat Marisol. She'd decided to come to the game after all. When she saw Nick looking over, she smiled and gave a quick, almost sheepish wave, as if embarrassed he'd spotted her. Later she'd tell him that she'd snuck up there when Nick was batting, so as not to distract him.

She didn't distract him now.

But the man sitting next to her did.

Marisol's dad.

Dressed in his police uniform.

12

BEN COULD SEE THAT SOMETHING WASN'T RIGHT WITH NICK, AND called time out with the home-plate ump, even though Nick hadn't thrown a pitch yet in the bottom of the sixth.

"'Sup?" he said.

"Marisol's here," Nick said, keeping his voice low and doing his best not to make eye contact with her in the stands.

"I told you she might come," Ben said. "No biggie."

Then he attempted to make a joke out of it.

"What're you worried about—she gonna hit against you?"

Nick knew they were running out of time. Any minute the ump would tell them to break up the conversation.

"She's with her *dad*," Nick said. "And they're sitting with *my* dad."

Ben moved his eyes up to the bleachers inconspicuously. He didn't want to be obvious about it.

"They're just sitting, watching the game," he said.

"It just looks weird, that's all. Seeing a uniform so close to my dad."

"Don't psych yourself out," Ben said. "Just pitch."

Ben walked back to the plate and got behind the batter into his crouch. Nick proceeded to walk the Giants' right fielder on four straight pitches. Then walked their third baseman on five.

He couldn't remember the last time he'd walked two guys in a full game, let alone two in a row to start an inning.

First and second, nobody out.

Just like that, the Giants had the potential tying runs on base, and the top of their batting order ready to face Nick.

Coach Viera called time and jogged out to the mound. Nick knew he was coming to try to relax him. *Good luck with that,* he thought.

When Coach got to the mound, he squinted around the field as if trying to locate someone at Macombs Dam Park.

"Have you happened to see my starting pitcher? I seem to have misplaced him somehow."

"You mean like I've misplaced the strike zone?" Nick said.

"You tired?"

"No, sir."

"You want to come out?"

"No, sir!" Nick said, more emphatically this time.

"Then don't make me take you out," Coach said. He gave Nick a quick pat on the shoulder and left.

Nick inhaled deeply. His mom suggested breathing in, holding it for a few seconds, then exhaling slowly when he needed to relax. At the same time, he tried to decide what was bothering him more: the three people in the bleachers or the two guys on base.

But there was one other thought pinballing inside his head now, vying for space in his already crowded brain. How long had Marisol been watching him tonight? He didn't know whether she'd seen him pitching at his best. But it would be too embarrassing to think she'd only seen him at his worst.

He threw ball one to their catcher, José. The pitch wasn't even in the vicinity of a strike.

Ben came out of his crouch and threw the ball hard back to Nick. His way of telling Nick to snap out of it. They both knew that if he walked the bases loaded, the next time Coach came to the mound would be to take the ball away.

Nick couldn't bear to look over at the bleachers, so he decided just to focus on Ben instead. Then he threw the best fastball he'd thrown all night. José was taking all the way. He was going to make Nick throw him a strike, and Nick had thrown him a strike, right down the middle.

Nick threw José another fastball just like that, same place. José swung and missed for strike two. Then another swing and miss at a high fastball for strike three.

When Nick was going good, Ben liked to say he was "dealing." Nick was dealing now. Kept dealing, too, as he struck out Carlo Rotella on three pitches.

Eric Dobbs coming to the plate now.

Nick knew that this was the game for him. *His* game. His best stuff—he hoped—against their best hitter.

A swing and a miss from Eric.

Then he took a ball.

One-and-one. Nick got a call with the next pitch, a borderline strike on the inside corner, the kind of call Eric hadn't gotten since way back in the top of the first.

One-and-two.

He saw Ben nod once behind the plate.

Nick threw another high fastball. It would have been

ball two, but Eric swung and missed—by a lot—for strike three.

Inning over. Nick knew that was it for the night. He resisted the urge to look over his shoulder one last time as he walked to the Blazers' bench, remembering an expression his dad had told him once. It was something an old Major League Baseball pitcher named Satchel Paige was famous for saying.

Don't look back. Something might be gaining on you.

13

KENNY LOCKE, THEIR CLOSER, DID HIS JOB IN THE BOTTOM OF THE seventh, getting out the last three Giants hitters in order. The Blazers won, 2–0. In the handshake line behind the pitcher's mound, Nick made it to Eric Dobbs, and said, "You pitched great tonight," putting out his hand. Eric brushed it so lightly it was like they hadn't made contact at all.

"Next time" was all Eric said, and moved on.

Ben was behind Nick in the line. When they were through shaking hands, Ben said, "Can't believe you and Eric didn't hug it out there."

Diego walked over. He'd seen what happened with Nick and Eric, too.

"Think we should invite Eric for ice cream?" Diego said.

"He said 'next time,'" Nick said. "The only way there's a next time is if we meet them in the championship game."

"If they're good enough to get there," Ben said. "They couldn't even put up one run against us."

"We have to be good enough, too," Nick said, trying not to get cocky.

"We are," said Ben.

Diego put a hand on Ben's shoulder. "You do have a way with words, my friend."

The three of them were standing behind the mound together. Nick looked over and saw his dad and Marisol with her dad waiting for him in front of the bleachers.

"Just gonna stand here?" Ben said. "Or are you gonna go talk to her?"

"Talking to her is one thing," Nick said. "Talking to her dad is what scares me."

"Thank him for coming to watch you pitch," Diego said. "And maybe throw in a thank-you for having such a pretty daughter."

"That's your idea of helping?" Nick said, pulling off his hat and running a hand through his hair.

"What do I know?" Diego said. "But you gotta admit, that was some funny stuff right there."

"We could come with you," Ben offered.

Nick took one of those long, slow, deep breaths.

"No," he said. "I got this." He was not sure that he did.

He walked over to them, more nervous now than he'd been in the bottom of the sixth. But his dad looked perfectly relaxed standing there next to a policeman. *If he can act this way*, Nick told himself, *so can I.*

"Hey, Dad," Nick said, coming in for a sideways hug.

Then he immediately put out his hand to Marisol's father, as if Officer Eddie Pérez were the last one in the handshake line, and said, "Thank you for coming to watch our game, sir."

"Hey," Marisol said. "What about me? Officer *Dad* was late getting home from work. I was so afraid we were going to miss the game, I didn't even let him change out of his uniform."

Nick smiled at her, because he couldn't help himself.

"Thank you *all* for coming," he added.

"A few nervous moments there at the end," Victor said. "You seemed to have lost your command out of nowhere."

"You sound like an old catcher," Nick said.

"Because I *am* an old catcher."

"But you got it back in no time, Nick," Marisol's dad said. "Wish I had a fastball like yours when I was growing up. Might be wearing a pinstriped uniform instead of this one." He gestured to his navy-blue shirt, with the NYPD badge sewn onto the sleeve.

"You were going for the corners," Marisol said. "Like I do on the court."

Victor García smiled at Officer Pérez. "The girl knows her baseball."

"More than she lets on," Officer Pérez said.

Nick was perplexed. "She tells me all the time she doesn't really like it," he said.

Look at you, he thought. *Just standing here chopping it up with a policeman, as if that's the most natural thing in the world.*

"Well," Marisol's dad said, "I have to say, I've never seen my daughter so invested in baseball as when you were getting those strikeouts at the end."

He was tall, the way Marisol was going to be tall, with the same golden-brown eyes and chestnut hair. Nick could see her face in his.

"*Daddy!*" she said, tugging on his arm.

"Did I just break a law by telling the truth?" her dad said.

"*Yes!*" Marisol said, her cheeks suddenly turning pink.

"Well," said Officer Pérez, putting out his wrists, "maybe you ought to cuff me and arrest me."

Nick observed his dad, to see if he reacted to jokes about handcuffs and arrests. All Victor García did was smile politely. But it wasn't genuine, Nick could tell.

"Nick," Officer Pérez said, "I was telling your dad that our families should have dinner together at our apartment sometime."

Nick's dad nodded and said, "We'll have to set something up soon."

Then they were all back to talking about the game and what a fine pitcher's duel it turned out to be.

"The Giants' pitcher's name is Eric," Nick said. "He's one of the best in the league." It was like he was reading off a script. Saying what he thought he should say, even though inside, he believed himself to be the better pitcher.

"One of the best, but not as good as you were tonight," Officer Pérez said.

"Daddy," Marisol whined, "are you and Nick just going to stand here and talk about baseball all night?"

"Fine with me," her dad said, grinning down at Nick.

Officer Pérez might want to, but Nick surely didn't, and he was grateful to Marisol for cutting their conversation short. He'd stayed behind longer than he'd planned to, and the rest of the team was already assembled, ready to get ice cream. So he told Marisol that he needed to go get with his teammates.

"See you tomorrow?" Marisol said, as if they'd already made plans. It had sounded like a question, but they both knew it wasn't.

"See you," Nick said.

Marisol put out her fist and Nick gave it a quick bump.

"Not a bad game," she said, "for baseball."

Then she and her dad began walking toward the lights and

noise of Yankee Stadium. As soon as they were out of earshot, Nick said to his dad, "We're going to dinner at a cop's house?"

"He's your friend's father," Victor replied. "And he asked. It would have sounded odd to refuse."

"He may be Marisol's dad," Nick said, "but he's still a police officer."

"I know," Victor García said.

"All it would take is one of them," Nick said, still wondering why his dad was being so blasé about the whole exchange.

"I'm aware of that, Nick," Victor García said, sternly reminding his son who the parent was.

Nick calmed down a bit. "I've seen Officer Pérez plenty of times before," he said. "Just never in uniform. It scared me; that's why I lost my command out there."

Victor García got down on one knee in front of Nick and grabbed his arms on both sides. "You let me do the worrying, okay? You just focus out there and play your heart out. That's all I want from you. You got it?"

Nick nodded, but mostly because it was easier to agree than to fight back. Telling him not to worry was like telling him to stop throwing fastballs. It was never going to happen.

Finally, his dad stood up and slapped a hand to Nick's back. "Go be with your teammates."

It should have been a perfect baseball night. Their third win of the season, Nick outpitching his biggest rival, and Marisol showing up to watch.

So why didn't it feel that way?

14

AMELIA WAS ALREADY ASLEEP BY THE TIME NICK GOT HOME.

He opened her bedroom door a sliver to check on her, but she was on her side facing away from the door, so he couldn't see her face. Though if he could, he was sure she'd look as peaceful as ever. If she worried about the same things Nick did, including her own health, she never showed it.

He had asked his mom one time if there was a chance Amelia could die from lupus. It was just the two of them seated at the kitchen table, where they did their best talking.

She'd put a hand across the table, over Nick's.

"Someday," Graciela García said, "when Amelia is even older than Mrs. Gurriel, your sister may die *with* lupus. But she is not going to die *of* it."

"But there's no cure, right? So she'll always have to suffer?"

"She'll always have to deal with it on some level, but that doesn't mean she can't have a good life."

"She never even complains," Nick said.

His mom let out a big laugh. "Ay, mi amor, of course she does!" she said. "Just not in front of you. She saves it for her mother."

Nick closed his sister's door now and thought about watching the rest of the Yankee game in the living room, then decided to listen instead.

He closed his bedroom door and lay down underneath the Michael Arroyo poster above his bed. Then he set the radio to the game, adjusting the volume so as not to wake Amelia on the other side of the wall.

Amelia might complain to their mom sometimes. But Nick never saw her feeling sorry for herself. He often had to remind himself to be the same way.

Nick rolled over on his side, propped his head up on an elbow, and looked up at Michael Arroyo's left arm coming forward, straight over the top.

Michael may have been Nick's baseball hero, but he was far from the only hero in Nick's life.

Now that the Blazers were well into the tournament, and because there were other summer leagues using the field at Macombs Dam Park, Coach Viera told them there'd be fewer daytime practices between games. Instead, they'd gather in the evenings, once he finished work as one of the store managers at the Staples on White Plains Road.

But Nick told Coach he'd try to organize some informal practices during the day if they could find a free field.

The Blazers had just finished their final practice of the week the Thursday after the Giants game.

Ben and Diego were the last two players on the field; everybody else had gone home. They were racing each other across the outfield. Getting after it. Looking like Bronx Blazers in every possible way.

"I know what this tournament means to all of you," Coach

said to Nick on the bench. "And I know how much it means to you especially."

Nick sat, listening.

"But if things work out, there's more in it for you."

"You know me," Nick said. "I'm only interested in winning the championship. And getting to sit together at a Yankee game."

That was another tournament detail arranged between the Dream League and the Yankees: the players on the winning team would get to sit in the fancy seats close to the field.

"I hear you," Coach said. "But that doesn't mean I can't live vicariously through you. So many times I've thought of what it would have been like to stand on that mound when I was a boy."

Nick laughed, but he was nothing if not superstitious. "It just feels like when you make a wish before blowing out the candles on your birthday cake. If you say the wish aloud, it won't come true."

"That doesn't mean we can't say it to ourselves," Coach Viera said.

"Maybe sometimes we do that more than we should," Nick said, thinking of Amelia and knowing he should stay humble. No use counting your chickens before they hatch.

Then he met up with Diego and Ben, and the three of them walked across 161st Street to the Stadium. It was a short practice tonight, so the Yankee game would still be in the early innings. They walked up the steps of Babe Ruth Plaza, hearing the voices of John Sterling and Suzyn Waldman from inside.

Diego started to say something, but Nick held up a hand.

"Listen," he said.

"What? We hear them all the time across the street," Diego blurted.

"They're talking about Michael Arroyo," Nick said, shushing him.

Ben looked sideways at Nick. "He's pitching tonight. I'd think that much would be obvious . . ."

"Yeah, figured you'd be running home to watch," Diego added.

"I will," Nick said. "But it sounds like he's trying to pitch himself out of trouble."

They listened to the announcers. It was bases loaded in the top of the third. According to John Sterling, there had been a single, an error, a walk after two were out.

"Nobody's really hit a ball hard for the Phillies in this inning," John Sterling said. "But there's no place to put the batter, and he's behind in the count, two-and-one."

"He needs to throw a strike here," Suzyn Waldman said.

"He will," Nick answered, as if she could hear him.

"Here's the pitch," John Sterling said. Then his voice rose an octave as he said, *"Cut on and missed!"*

The cheer from inside was loud enough to permeate the walls of the Stadium. Enough that Nick felt as if he were watching the game from inside, instead of standing outside it.

They could hear the two-strike sound Yankee Stadium could make in a big moment, the crowd telling Michael Arroyo they wanted him to get a strikeout and end the inning.

"Here's . . . the . . . pitch," John Sterling said, dragging out the words the way he did.

Nick waited.

"He . . . struck . . . him . . . out!" John Sterling yelled, before they heard the crowd go wild.

"Now *that* was some high heat," Suzyn Waldman said.

"Was it ever," John Sterling agreed. Then he recapped the last play. After two and a half innings, the Yankees still led the Philadelphia Phillies, 1–0.

"Can we go now?" Diego said in his whiny voice. "If you hurry home, you can watch your guy pitch the top of the fourth yourself."

Nick surrendered, and they made for home.

After dropping Diego at his building, Nick split from Ben at his.

He was walking up Grand Concourse toward his apartment when he saw a van marked IMMIGRATION AND CUSTOMS ENFORCEMENT parked in front of a neighboring building. Five or six uniformed people piled out, seemingly led by one man.

The man Nick's sure he had seen staring at his building only days earlier.

15

THEY WORE DARK-BLUE VESTS THAT LOOKED TO NICK LIKE THE bulletproof ones you saw people wearing in TV shows. ICE and POLICE were written on the back. They were mostly men, but Nick saw at least one woman in the group.

Nick was sure that the man in charge *was* the man he'd seen staring up at his building that night from across the street. There had been six floors separating them, along with the Grand Concourse, and of course, tonight he was wearing a baseball cap.

But this was the same man.

Nick just knew it.

Now the man directed his crew as they assembled on the sidewalk, motioning for them to fan out on either side of the entrance, and waving some of them around back to the building at 164th and Grand Concourse.

Nick wanted to run, but he was frozen in place, as he watched what his mom called the "immigrant nightmare" playing out for someone else's family, only a stone's throw from where Nick lived.

Two men walked inside the building now. Another man and the woman took up positions on the sidewalk, holding back the crowd that was beginning to form.

There was another crowd gathering on Nick's side of the Grand Concourse, most of them adults, but some kids, too.

"Who do you think they came for?" asked a woman behind Nick.

A man next to her said, "You mean, who did they come for *this time*?"

"I guess," the woman said.

"I don't know. But we're about to find out." He wore a faded blue cap with the Yankees NY on the front.

These weren't people coming out just to witness a spectacle, Nick observed. These were neighborhood folks, genuinely worried about their community.

"What do you think happened?" the woman asked. Nick wished she'd stop asking so many questions. Especially ones he didn't want answers to.

"Probably a repeat offender," the man said. "When they come out in force like this, it's usually for somebody who's been arrested before."

Nick felt light-headed all of a sudden. He thought he might faint.

"Which law?" the woman said.

"The law against being an immigrant," the man said facetiously.

"Not all of us are undocumented," the woman argued.

"Doesn't stop them from looking at us all the same these days."

Across the Grand Concourse, they waited to see what would happen next. Nick kept telling himself to leave, get out of here. Just go home. He played out scenarios in his head. Like that the lead ICE official would suddenly notice Nick and come walking in his direction.

But he couldn't make himself leave. He had only ever heard about raids like this, like for Mr. Romero, whom he overheard his parents discussing in the kitchen that night. Now he was seeing one with his own eyes.

The minutes ticked by until Nick heard a commotion coming from the crowd closest to the building. Two men in vests came outside with a young man between them, head down, hands cuffed behind his back.

Right behind him was a young woman, screaming and crying as the man in handcuffs was escorted to the van.

Nick couldn't understand what she was saying in Spanish, the words flowing out of her hot and fast. But there was no mistaking the sentiment. Whoever this man was to her, whether a brother, a friend, a husband, or something else, she loved him, and it tore her apart to watch him being taken away from her.

The woman broke away from the female ICE official restraining her and ran toward the van, before two more vests blocked her.

The woman yelled again, reaching a hand hopelessly between their arms.

Now the ICE man in charge, the one Nick had identified as the man from the street, turned to view the crowd across the way. Nick had moved to the front by then.

There's no way he's looking at me, Nick thought. *He doesn't even know me. Now you really are acting crazy.*

But he ducked his head anyway, and weaved among the masses, squeezing himself behind one of the old neighborhood men.

Of course, the old man decided that very moment to start yelling across traffic.

"What are you looking at?" the old man shouted, his face angry and red.

Nick sidestepped to put some space between them, and to further shield himself from view.

"You wanna come over here and arrest us all?" the old man said, egging them on.

"You think we're all criminals if we look the way we do?" he continued, shaking a fist at the enforcement officers. "I don't think you got enough handcuffs in there for all of us."

The ICE agent didn't answer. His face remained emotionless, almost as if he were telling the people across the street that he didn't make the laws, he just enforced them.

It had suddenly become a long night. Now Nick just wanted it all to be over. He wanted to see the blue vests get into the van and drive off and leave them alone. Maybe he would find out later why the young man had been arrested in the first place.

Finally, the old man stopped yelling. A handful of neighbors came outside to console the young woman, whose crying now simmered to a soft weeping. The blue vests climbed inside the van and closed the back doors from the inside. The head officer walked around to the driver's side and took one last look at the old man, who stared back at him defiantly. Then he hopped in behind the wheel, slammed the door, and took off down the road, leaving everyone on Grand Concourse in his wake.

As soon as the van was out of sight, Nick ran toward his building.

Ran without once looking over his shoulder, never stopping until he was through the front door and up the stairs.

He wanted to stop on Mrs. Gurriel's floor; tell her that he'd just seen the future, too, but it wasn't the happy future she envisioned for Nick, or Amelia, or their family.

He didn't, though. And he didn't realize he was crying until he made it inside the apartment.

16

THE FOUR OF THEM SAT AT THE KITCHEN TABLE: NICK, HIS PARENTS, and Amelia. Nick had just finished recounting what he'd witnessed on the way home.

Nick's mom said she heard about it after receiving a text from a friend who lived in the building.

"The young man is from Ecuador," Graciela García said. "He'd been deported once before, after defending his wife from a man harassing her on the street. But somehow he made it back into the country. He still had a record, though. That's how ICE and the police were able to track him."

"It doesn't sound like a very serious crime," Amelia said, "defending his wife."

"For people like us," Victor García said, "all crimes are treated as serious crimes now, no matter how minor."

"Even if all you were trying to do was get to a job interview," Nick said.

His dad nodded gravely.

"Why do they bully people like this?" Nick asked in earnest.

"Because they can," his father replied.

"It could happen to you," Amelia said. It was what they were all thinking. Now she had said it.

"Yes," her dad said. "But it won't."

"But it could," she said. Nick was glad Amelia was speaking what he couldn't bring himself to say. Perhaps Amelia did share his fears.

"But it won't. I won't let it."

They sat in silence. This was a family conversation they'd had before, and Nick and Amelia always knew how it went. Their dad would reassure them he was being careful. He'd urge them to be cautious about whom they spoke to, whom they trusted, and to be suspicious of anyone they didn't know. Then he'd say he was hopeful that soon new politicians would take control of the government in Washington, DC, people who knew how much immigrants have contributed toward making America the kind of place where people want to come and live.

"I read something President Ronald Reagan once said," Victor García began. "He said, 'Anybody from any corner of the world can come to America to live and become an American.'"

"That man I saw being put into the van tonight—do you think he thought of himself that way?" Nick asked.

"He risked everything to come back here," his mom said. "I don't see how he could think of himself any other way."

There was nothing more to say, at least not tonight. Amelia went to her room. Nick went to his. He didn't know how the Yankee game ended, and for this one night, he didn't care.

Nick got ready for bed on autopilot. As he flicked off his light and closed his eyes, he saw the man in handcuffs, his wife crying, the old man, and the blue vests.

He lay there like that for a long time, knowing it would be hard for sleep to find him tonight.

He was still wide-awake when he heard the door creak open, and saw the silhouette of his father in the doorframe. With the light from the hallway, Nick could see him wearing a gray T-shirt and running shorts.

"I am so sorry you had to see that," Victor García said.

Nick felt a lump begin to rise up inside his throat, but he forced himself to swallow it down. He didn't want to feel sorry for himself. Amelia never did, and Nick wasn't going to, either.

He wondered, in the dim light, if his dad could see him squeeze his eyes shut before opening them again, willing the tears away.

"I am so sorry," his dad continued, "that I am putting our family through this." He sighed. "My children are citizens and their parents are not. Qué mundo."

"You did nothing wrong."

"But I did," his dad said, his voice soft.

Nick didn't want to blame his dad for one mistake, and found it extremely unfair that he'd have to pay for that mistake every day of his life.

"Things will get better," his dad said. "We all have to keep believing that."

"It's so hard sometimes."

"I know," Victor García said. "One of the definitions of faith is believing in what you cannot see."

"I know what I saw tonight," Nick said.

At the kitchen table earlier, Nick had hesitated to tell his family what he knew about the head ICE agent—he didn't want to scare anyone. But in the end, he decided it was best if someone else knew. It was funny, Nick thought: "ICE Man" made him sound like somebody who belonged in a comic book. Or maybe an Avengers movie. A bad guy masquerading as one of the good guys.

"You're sure it was the man you saw outside our building?" Victor asked now in Nick's bedroom.

"Pretty sure, Dad."

"If you see him again, anywhere in our neighborhood, you tell me," Victor García said. "If I am at work, you call me or tell your mother."

"Okay."

"Now go to sleep."

"I can't."

They were on familiar ground now.

"Funny. You've always managed in the past," his dad said, before closing the door, leaving Nick in darkness.

It wasn't until he awoke the next morning that he found out the Yankees won and Michael Arroyo hadn't given up another run before leaving the game after the eighth inning.

There were so few things to count on these days: the love of his family, his ability to throw a baseball, friends he could trust.

And he could count on Michael Arroyo.

Michael had once been afraid in the Bronx the way Nick was afraid now. Maybe Michael had needed faith, too. Faith to believe he'd ever have the kind of life he had now.

Nick tried to envision that kind of life for himself. The life he should have. But all he could see, even in his dreams, was the ICE Man, standing between him and Yankee Stadium.

17

MARISOL CALLED THE NEXT DAY TO TELL NICK SHE WAS MEETING A friend at the tennis court the following morning, and asked if he wanted to come along.

"It's about time I see you in action," he said.

"Took the words right outta my mouth."

Most of the time she played at the Stadium Tennis Center, a big place with indoor and outdoor courts at 152nd Street near the Harlem River.

"Do I have to carry your rackets?" Nick asked when he met her on the corner of 161st and Grand Concourse.

"Do you ask me to carry your bat and glove?" was her retort.

"Stupid question, huh?"

"Nah, it was cute," Marisol said, and Nick could feel himself blushing all the way to his ears.

Marisol played tennis almost every day. When she wasn't taking lessons with her coach or playing matches, she hit with her friend Nicole, who also played singles on their summer travel team. They played more matches than the Blazers did games in their tournament. But at the end, the top two teams would play a championship match at the Billie Jean King National Tennis Center, which hosted the US Open, right across the street from the Mets' ballpark, Citi Field.

"I can't even imagine," Marisol said to Nick as they made the walk to the Stadium Tennis Center, "what it would be like playing in the stadium there."

"I can imagine it," Nick said. "Totally."

"I guess it would kinda be similar to you pitching inside Yankee Stadium," Marisol said knowingly.

They were waiting for the light at 155th Street. Nick bristled at her words, and turned to face her.

"You know about the MVP award?" he said incredulously.

"I know," she said, with a teasing twinkle in her eye.

"Who told you?" Nick said. "Ben or Diego?"

"Neither," she said. "One of the guys my dad works with is on the board of the Dream League. He told my dad."

Great, Nick thought. *Like I need another cop knowing my name.*

"Anyway," Marisol said, "my dad was the one who told me you might get the chance to throw out the first pitch. He said now we both have something extra to play for this summer."

"I'm not the only player in the league who could win the MVP," Nick said, trying to play it smooth.

"But won't you have the best chance if your team wins the championship?" she asked.

"It might help," Nick said. "But sometimes they pick a player who's not on the best team. Eric Dobbs, another pitcher, is really, *really* good. There's this big guy, Benny Alvarez, who I'm sure is gonna lead the league in home runs."

"But if you're the best pitcher on the best team, it's got to be you, right?"

Nick shook his head.

"Doesn't always work that way," he said. "Mike Trout, who plays for the Angels in the big leagues, has won multiple MVPs, and the Angels weren't close to being the best team when he did."

"Well, if I had a vote, you'd get it," Marisol said.

Nick smiled. "Thanks," he said. "Hope the coaches who vote feel the same way."

Then he dropped the subject and promised to focus on her tennis for the rest of the day.

Nick couldn't believe how big the Stadium Tennis Center was: twelve courts side by side under a dome, with more courts outside. Nicole was waiting for Marisol on one of the outdoor courts. She said it was too nice a day to play inside. Nicole had a long blonde ponytail swinging down her back and was even taller than Nick. Marisol tied her own dark hair into a braid before introducing them courtside.

"So *you're* the pitcher I've been hearing so much about," Nicole said in singsong.

"Oh, *have* you?" Nick said, grinning at Marisol.

"Ni*cole*," Marisol said. "Try to remember that you're supposed to be my *friend*?"

"Did I say something wrong?" Nicole said, covering her mouth in feigned embarrassment.

"You'll find out as soon as we're on the court, Miss Chatty," Marisol said.

"Bring it."

"I always do."

Nick didn't follow tennis, and probably knew less about it

than Marisol knew about baseball. But he only had to watch for a few minutes to appreciate how much athleticism and focus was involved. His head whipped back and forth to each side of the net, watching Marisol and Nicole going at it. He was impressed by how hard they hit, and noticed they put a spin on the ball just like Nick did when he secretly practiced throwing curves. Marisol had been right about one thing: in tennis, the action never let up for very long.

But it wasn't just tennis that was amazing to him. *Marisol* was amazing. Nick could tell, even without knowing much about the sport, that Nicole was a good player. But she was no Marisol Pérez.

She was like a power pitcher and a power hitter all in one, and she never seemed to get tired, running after the ball and trying to move Nicole from side to side. She came sprinting in for balls near the net, then immediately backed up to the baseline when Nicole managed to get a ball over her head.

Every once in a while, she gave out a whoop or shook a fist when she hit a winner. Nick never got the feeling that she was trying to show up her friend. It was more a feeling of pride for herself.

She and Nicole were doing what Nick, Ben, and Diego did in baseball: getting after it.

Marisol had explained the scoring in tennis to Nick on the way over, and he thought he had it down, even if it made absolutely no sense to him: 15–love, 15–30, 30–40. Deuce.

"What's wrong with one-zero, two-zero, three-zero?" Nick said.

"It kind of started out this way in France, in olden times," Marisol explained. "I read up on the history of the whole 'love' thing."

"Love?" *Now* there's *a word*, Nick thought.

"It had something to do with zeros being the shape of eggs and the French word for eggs sounding like 'love,'" Marisol said, throwing her hands up. "Hey, it wasn't my idea."

"But you said that when there's a tiebreaker, you just count up the points until somebody gets to seven and wins by two."

"Maybe it's because the tiebreaker was invented in America!"

"You know what else was invented in America?" Nick said.

"What?"

"Baseball."

"Does everything come back to baseball with you?" she said teasingly.

He grinned. "Nah. I'm totally a tennis guy now."

"Ha!"

"Hey! I could surprise you," Nick said.

She raised an eyebrow. "I'll bet you're full of surprises."

"What's that mean?" he said.

"Just throwing that out there," she said. "Like a curveball."

Nick was absorbed in the match, rooting for Marisol but trying not to be obvious about it. When a ball rolled off the court, Nick acted as a ball boy, running after it. It was all fun, and Nick enjoyed the reprieve from worrying about what happened two nights ago. Like the anxious part of his brain got a chance to shut down for a few hours. It felt good to get out of himself and into a sport that wasn't his own.

Marisol won the first set against Nicole, and Nicole came back to win the next 6–4. Finally they decided to play a tiebreaker, which Marisol ended up winning 7–5, passing Nicole, who'd come to the net, with one last screaming forehand. After the move, Nick couldn't help himself. He stood up and applauded.

"Guess we know who you were pulling for, baseball man," Nicole teased.

"I root for him when he plays," Marisol said, trying to avoid the awkwardness of before by saving Nick the embarrassment.

Nick didn't care how long the walk home took from the tennis center. He was with Marisol. He knew he would always stress a little in her presence, nervous something might slip out of his mouth that he'd regret. But he couldn't deny that being with her made him happy.

Something was nagging at him, though. And maybe it was that he wasn't being 100 percent truthful with her. She didn't know the whole story, the part of himself he reserved for his family, and sometimes Ben and Diego. Nick didn't feel as if he were deceiving her, exactly. His father did tell him to be cautious about divulging the family's personal information. But Marisol felt like family. It didn't seem right to keep things from her.

But he couldn't tell her about his dad's crime. Marisol was a policeman's daughter, and Nick was unsure about police protocol. If Nick told her about his dad's past and all the rest of it, maybe it was Officer Pérez's duty to tell his superiors. Or maybe he'd be obligated to simply arrest Nick's dad himself. Nick couldn't compromise his own family like that, and didn't want to put Marisol in a difficult position.

They were getting near Yankee Stadium when Marisol said, "Did you hear about the man they arrested last night?"

Nick's face grew hot. "You know about that?"

"My mom said everybody in the neighborhood is talking about it," Marisol said. "Your parents must know."

"I was there," Nick said.

"Are you serious?" Marisol said. "You saw it happen?"

"Yeah." Nick wished Marisol would drop the subject, but that was highly unlikely.

"It must have been crazy," she said.

"It was sad, actually," Nick said. "The man's wife—at least I think it was his wife—was there, too, crying while they took him away."

"But he'd been arrested before, right?" Marisol said, like it was a simple matter. "My dad always says that if you got arrested, you did *something*."

Nick's stomach twisted up inside. Marisol always saw everything in plain black and white. To Nick, it was much more complicated than that.

They were walking past Nick's field now. Nobody was playing, and Nick wasn't sure whether there was a game scheduled for later. But anytime he came here and the field wasn't in use, it always felt like a waste of a perfectly good ball field.

Nick told Marisol what he had learned about the man from Ecuador. How he'd been deported for defending his wife, and came back to America to be with her.

"But it all started because he broke the law," Marisol said.

Nick didn't want to be having this conversation with her, afraid more than ever that he might say too much. He wanted so badly to explain to Marisol that not every crime is done with malice. But he stopped himself before the words could come flying out of him.

What he did say: "I don't even know the man, but to me it doesn't seem like what he did should be enough to ruin their lives."

Marisol, rackets tucked in the case under her arm, stopped now, behind the screen near home plate, a curious look on her face.

"You seem to have given this a lot of thought, for someone you don't even know," she said.

"Like you said," Nick replied, "everybody was talking about it."

"Uh-huh."

They took a right at 161st and walked underneath the subway tracks. When the roar of the train pulling into the station subsided, Marisol said, "You can confide in me, you know. If there's anything you want to tell me. I'm good at keeping secrets."

"If I tell you, then they won't be secrets," Nick said, trying to make a joke but also desperate to change the subject again.

"For real?" Marisol's face grew serious. "I'd be really hurt if you kept something big from me."

And probably end up hating me, too, Nick thought.

"Okay! For real," he said, ready to end this conversation. "Now, let's talk about funny things."

"Like what?" she said.

"Like that little squeak you make when you lean into a shot."

He tried to imitate it, and thought he'd done a pretty decent job. She tried to punch his arm, but he dodged her and ran up the sidewalk. Marisol chased after him—Marisol, who didn't want him keeping secrets from her.

Nick didn't want to think about what would happen someday when she found out he had. How big a crime would the policeman's daughter think he had committed?

18

NICK'S PARENTS WERE COMING TO THE GAME TONIGHT, AND SO WAS Amelia. That morning, she'd told Nick she was feeling well enough to come. When Nick asked about the sun, Amelia said she had a new hat so big it would be like sitting under a palm tree. Marisol had a late tennis practice, but said she'd at least catch the last few innings on the way home.

Things had been calm in the neighborhood for the past few days. Nick hadn't heard of any further ICE raids in the South Bronx, and there was no sight of the ICE Man since that night. Nick stopped thinking about the raid, because Amelia told him there was no point.

"It does no good to worry about things you can't control," Amelia said before Nick left to pick up Ben and Diego.

"You're telling me you don't worry about what could happen?" Nick said.

"Of course I do," she said. "But we have to be strong. Don't let it dominate your life."

"I wish I were as strong as you," Nick said.

"Oh, stop it!" Amelia said, surprising them both with the sharpness of her tone. "Stop talking about me like I'm some kind of saint. I'm not a precious artifact in a museum you have to tiptoe around and handle with white gloves. Don't treat me like

I'm somehow better than everyone else because I'm living with a disease."

Nick was taken aback. He always thought he was making her feel better by telling her how strong she was. He never imagined it could have the opposite effect.

"I just want you to feel better," he choked out. "Is that so wrong?"

"That's the thing, Nick. I don't think of myself as being sick," Amelia said.

"I don't understand."

"This is just who I am," Amelia said. "The way you're a baseball player, or Dominican American, or a seventh grader. We all deal with different things in our lives, but we gotta take the bad with the good."

Nick plopped down on the couch. "Are you sure you're only one year older than me?"

"I have a lot of time to think about things," Amelia said, sitting beside him.

She took out her phone. "And right now, the only thing you should be thinking about is getting your butt to that field and throwing heat."

"You think I will?"

"I know you will," she said.

The Dream League tournament, Nick and his buddies had decided, was going way too fast.

They were at the field, getting ready to play the Braves, trying to maintain an undefeated record with only a handful of games left before the championship.

"This whole thing is like ice cream," Diego said.

Ben poked Nick. "This ought to be good. Like, really good."

"Seriously," Diego said. "Check this out."

Nick groaned. "Do we have a choice?"

"Playing this tournament *is* like eating an ice-cream cone," Diego said.

"What kind?" Ben said.

"Whatever your favorite kind is—that's not the point."

"One scoop or two?" Nick said.

"Do you guys want to hear this or not?" Diego said, visibly chafed.

"'Want' is a strong word," said Ben.

"So you start eating the ice-cream cone," Diego said, "and you can't believe how great it tastes. But you wanna make it last, so you tell yourself to slow down. Except you *can't* slow down! Because if you do, the ice cream is going to melt. See where I'm going with this?"

"As long as you do," Ben said. "That's what matters."

"I'm trying to make a point here!"

Nick snorted. "You sure about that?"

Diego glared at him.

"My *point*," he continued, "is that sometimes you can't slow fun down no matter how hard you try."

"Or it'll melt," Ben said in monotone.

"Exactly!" Diego said, relieved somebody finally got it. "You just have to enjoy the ride."

"So . . . two scoops?" Ben joked.

"And what about toppings?" Nick added.

"You guys just won't admit that I come up with some genius stuff sometimes," Diego said. "So go ahead, have your fun."

"Winning would be fun," said Nick.

"I like our chances tonight," Ben said.

"Do you know who's pitching for the Braves?" Nick asked.

"No," Ben said. "But I know who's pitching for us."

Nick was starting tonight. The schedule over the next couple of weeks only gave Nick a few starts, so that if the Blazers wound up playing for the championship, Nick could pitch that game with more than a week's rest.

The ball felt great coming out of Nick's hand as he loosened up behind the bench, and even better on the mound taking warm-up pitches before the Braves batted in the top of the first.

As the Blazers' infielders threw the ball around one last time before the game started, Nick darted his eyes up to the bleachers. There, in the second row from the top, sat his mom, his dad, and Amelia wearing her wide-brimmed hat. For a long time, Nick had felt alone in his fears, but Amelia was right. Everyone had their issues. It all came down to how you chose to deal with them.

Nick proceeded to walk the Braves' leadoff man on four pitches, not one of them close to being a strike. He finally threw a strike to Jeff Coyle, the Braves' third baseman, but then Jeff ripped a single right past Nick's glove and up the middle.

Nick went to a full count on the Braves' third hitter, and then walked him, too.

Bases loaded, nobody out.

Nick saw Ben, still in his crouch, turn and say something to the home-plate ump. Probably asking for time. The ump nodded, and Ben took a step out from behind the plate.

Nick held up a glove, stopping him. He didn't want to talk right now, not even to Ben. He didn't want a pep talk. He just wanted to figure things out himself.

The cleanup hitter for the Braves was their starting pitcher, Sammy Diaz. He was on Nick's team in the spring league, and when he wasn't pitching, he was a terrific shortstop, one who could really hit.

"You got this," Ronnie Lester called out from second base.

Right now, Nick thought, *I got nothing.*

Sammy took Nick's first pitch for a strike. *I would have been taking, too*, Nick thought. It was what you did when the pitcher couldn't find the plate. Coach always told him to stay in the moment. Just think about the next pitch. Only Nick couldn't stop his mind from racing. They were late in the tournament, and he couldn't afford to pitch this way. His dad liked to quote Yankee great Yogi Berra, who used to say, "It gets late early out there." Diego was right; the tournament was going fast. This game was getting away from him even faster. That was a fact, and so was this. If he didn't find his best stuff, the Blazers *wouldn't* make it to the big game.

He was throwing away his shot at the championship. Forget about making it across the street.

He threw what he thought was a good fastball to Sammy, but Sammy was sitting on it, and lined it over Melky's head at third, down the left-field line. By the time their left fielder, Max, ran the ball down, two runs were scored, and the Braves had runners on second and third.

Still nobody out.

Nick finally did get an out—a fly ball to left field from the next batter—but it was deep enough to score the runner from third on a sacrifice fly. So it was 3–0, Braves.

Then Nick lost the strike zone again, going to three-and-oh on the next batter.

He was doing the thing that Ben always cautioned him against early in the game. Overthrowing, squeezing the ball, trying too hard. But it wasn't like he had a choice. He had to hold them here. He couldn't let his team fall further behind.

When he threw ball four, making it first and second with one out, Coach Viera called time and came jogging out to the mound.

"I can get out of this," Nick said when Coach got to him.

"Might not be your night tonight," Coach said, grinning at Nick as if it was no big deal. "Happens to the best of 'em. Even happens to your man Arroyo from time to time."

"You're thinking of taking me out?" Nick said.

"This isn't just about one game," Coach said. "I don't want you to jeopardize your chances by letting them put up a really big number right here."

"Please don't take me out," Nick pleaded. "Let me pitch my way out of this."

Coach gave him a long, hard look. Nick could see the ump slowly moving out from behind the plate, letting them know their time was limited.

"Okay," Coach Viera said finally.

Nick let out the breath he was holding. "Thank you," he said.

"Thank me by starting the game over right here."

He took the ball from Nick's glove, rubbed it up quickly, stuffed it back in there, and left. Maybe the Blazers' tournament wasn't on the line here, but to Nick, it felt like it was. The next batter for the Braves, their first baseman, was Hassan Keyes, a big, left-handed hitter with power. Nick looked in to Ben for a sign, even though they only had two: fastball, changeup.

Ben wanted a changeup.

Hassan, who was expecting a fastball, was way ahead of the pitch, and off-balance. Swing and a miss. Strike one.

Ben called for another changeup.

Hassan missed again. Then swung and missed at the fastball Nick threw him for strike three. First strikeout of the night. *About time*, Nick thought.

One more out until Nick could put an end to this miserable opening. The Braves' second baseman was next. A little guy. Nick threw him the best fastball he'd thrown yet. The second baseman got a pretty good swing on it, but hit a one-hopper right back at Nick. He gloved the ball, ran halfway to first, then tossed it underhand to Darryl. The game stayed 3–0.

Nick took a deep breath, let it out, walked slowly back to the Blazers' bench. When he got there, Ben gave Nick's glove a big slap with his own.

"That was pitching right there," Ben said.

"I don't know what happened at the start," Nick admitted.

"I do," Ben said. "Baseball happened."

"It's why we play the game," Diego said, taking a few practice swings.

"You know something?" Nick said. "You're right."

"I am, aren't I?"

"Now go get a hit," Nick said.

"On it, Captain," Diego said, saluting.

Ben and Nick just shook their heads, laughing.

Sammy Diaz wasn't very tall, and didn't throw particularly hard. But he had terrific control, and the ability to move the ball from one side of the plate to the other. In the language of pitchers, Sammy could "paint."

He went to two-and-two on Diego. Diego still hadn't swung. He'd taken one strike on the outside corner, one Nick could tell by his body language Diego didn't think was a strike, and then one on the inside corner. It was almost as if he and Sammy were waiting each other out. But no pitcher wanted to walk the leadoff man. Nick sure hadn't wanted to. Sammy came right after Diego then: a fastball down the middle. Diego knew what to do with it, launching it over their center fielder's head, so hard Nick thought it might roll all the way to the adjacent field.

He ended up with a triple. Ben singled him home. Finally, the Blazers were on the board. Darryl doubled Ben home, and just like that, the score was 3–2. Sammy's inning was starting out the way Nick's had. If Nick's hope was to reset the clock at the top of the first, he was all but getting his wish served to him on a silver platter. Melky walked, and Nick hit the first pitch Sammy threw him for a hard single to right. Darryl scored.

Just like that, almost in a blink, they'd tied the Braves 3–3. Then Ronnie Lester singled home Melky, and suddenly, the Blazers had the lead. Sammy held them there, after a trip to the mound from his own coach. Blazers, 4–3.

Before they went out for the top of the second, Ben looked at Nick and said, "Do I even have to ask?"

"We have enough runs," Nick said, just loud enough for Ben to hear.

Diego came over. Usually he was the first Blazer back on the field. Now he was waiting for Nick and Ben.

"Let's make this the best win of the year," he said. "And this time I'm not joking."

They all touched gloves and took the field together.

Nick thought of the second inning as a fresh start, and made the most of it. For the next few innings, Nick erased the memory of the top of the first. Ben was right: baseball had happened tonight. Coach was right, too. It *hadn't* looked to be his night from those first few pitches. Regardless, Nick would *make* it his night. He knew pitching a shutout was impossible, so instead he did what all good pitchers were supposed to do: pitch to the scoreboard. He would hold the Braves at three runs for as long as he was out there. The Blazers were going to remain undefeated if Nick had anything to do with it. And he did. He may have pitched the worst inning of the tournament—the worst inning of his whole year, in fact. Now *he* was going to tough it out. Amelia was right: you had to accept the bad with the good, and take matters into your own hands.

He finally struck out the side in the top of the fourth. By then the Blazers had increased their lead to 6–3. His pitch count was high, though, because of all the pitches he'd front-loaded in the first inning, so Coach Viera told him he was coming out after the fifth.

"Or we could end your night right here," Coach said, "finishing on a high note."

"I want one more inning, Coach," Nick said. "Please?"

Coach nodded. "Give 'em a little something to remember us by, in case we end up playing them in the championship game."

"I started to have my doubts about making it there," Nick said.

"Not me."

"You were about to take me out," Nick said, incredulous.

"Nah," Coach said. "I just wanted to get your attention."

"Well, you succeeded," Nick said, laughing.

"As our friend Diego likes to say, I have my moments."

Nick didn't strike out the side in the fifth. He came close, though, striking out the first two batters he faced. He didn't need to check the score book to know he hadn't given up a single hit since the first. Nobody reached base, either. In Nick's mind, he was pitching an imperfect perfect game. Jeff Coyle was the Braves' last batter in the fifth. Nick got to oh-and-two, and thought he'd struck him out with some high heat. But somehow, Jeff got a tiny piece of the ball, and it ended up a few feet down the first baseline. Ben pounced on it and threw it to first to end the inning.

When Nick got to the bench, Coach motioned for him to sit down next to him.

"You pitched your best tonight after pitching your worst," he said. "That's something to be proud of."

"Didn't have much of a choice," Nick said, shrugging.

"But you learned something about yourself tonight. Sometimes you have to pitch as much with this"—he patted his own heart—"as you do with that," he said, pointing to Nick's arm.

After that, Coach didn't send him out to play second base, saying Nick was done for the night. He sat on the bench by himself after Coach ran out to third. A moment later, Amelia caught Nick's eye from the bleachers. She must have been watching his chat with Coach, because just then, she patted her own heart.

He smiled back.

Their closer, Kenny Locke, twice retired the Braves in order, throughout the sixth and seventh. The Blazers won, 6–3. They had to sweat it out for a while, but coming from behind made their win that much sweeter.

It was when they were in the handshake line that Nick noticed a man standing beyond the screen behind home plate.

He was sure it was the ICE Man.

Nick made his way through the line somehow, forcing himself to appear calm. Ben was behind him, as usual, and noticed him checking behind the plate every few seconds.

"What's up?" Ben said when they were through the line. "You look like you saw a ghost. And not the kind Derek Jeter talks about."

"Maybe I did," Nick said. "Be right back."

He ran past the Blazers' bench, toward the bleachers. His parents and Amelia were just starting to make their way down. Nick made eye contact with his dad and motioned with his hand for them to hurry. Maybe Victor García saw the same look on Nick's face that Ben had, because he took the steps down two at a time, making a beeline for his son.

"You don't look like someone who just won a game," his dad said. "What's bothering you?"

"The man I've been telling you about?" Nick said, panting, trying to get the words out. "The one I saw outside our building?"

Nick swallowed hard.

"Dad," he said, "he's here."

"Where?" Victor García said, setting a hand on Nick's shoulder.

Nick avoided making any sudden gestures that would tip the man off.

"Right behind the plate," Nick said to his dad.

"Where behind the plate?"

Nick turned around to look.

The man was gone.

19

NICK'S MOM GOT OFF EARLY FROM WORK, SO SHE MADE A SPECIAL pizza for dinner and even had time to bake bizcocho Dominicano, a light cake with meringue frosting, for dessert before leaving for Nick's game.

Normally this would have felt like a victory celebration, but a dark cloud settled over the table instead.

"You're sure it's the same man?" Nick's dad said.

"It's like I told you on the way home," Nick said. "He was wearing a cap when he arrested that man the other night, and it was pulled down over his eyes a little bit. But I'd bet anything it's the same man."

Victor's mouth was a hard line.

"But what would make him come to your game if he wasn't going to do anything?" Amelia asked, trying to puzzle it out.

Their parents shared a look across the table, hoping one would have a good answer.

"It makes no sense," Graciela said. "If he knows who we are, where we live, and even where Nick plays baseball, why wouldn't he just come knock on our door?"

A horrible feeling washed over Nick. What if he was wrong? If none of the facts were adding up, was it possible he was mistaken? No. It had to have been the ICE Man. Who else would have a reason for stalking Nick this way?

Nick's mom looked around the table, her eyes suddenly big and wide and rimmed in red. Nick didn't want her to cry. He hated it when she cried.

"I just want this to be over," she said, her voice full of hurt.

Victor put an arm around his wife. "But you know it may not be for a long time, and that's only if we are blessed with good fortune," Victor García said. "We have to put our trust in God until my beautiful daughter turns twenty-one."

By now Nick knew that Amelia's twenty-first birthday could be a kind of finish line for his parents. At that point, she'd have the opportunity to sponsor their parents for green cards, which would keep them in the country permanently, despite her father's arrest record. At least that's what Victor García's last lawyer had told him. It made no sense to Nick that his parents' fate hinged on his sister reaching the age of majority, but apparently that was the law.

Nick sat in silence. Amelia wouldn't turn twenty-one for another eight years. Nick would be twenty by then, his teen years well behind him. What would his life be like then? Would he be in college? Would he still be playing baseball?

Michael Arroyo was pitching for the Yankees by the time he was twenty. Carlos Arroyo, Michael's brother, was already his agent and manager.

"Eight years is almost as long as I've been alive," Nick said.

"We just have to keep believing we can get there," his dad said. "Together."

Victor García's strong hands were clasped on the table in front of him. Nick's mom put one hand over them now.

"Nick was right to point out the man as soon as he saw him,"

Victor said, "even if he doesn't turn out to be a threat. You know what they say on the subway, 'See something, say something'? That rule applies in our family as well."

With that, Nick and Amelia cleared away the last of the pizza and their mom brought out the chocolate cake.

"For the rest of the night," she said, "we're only going to talk about happy things."

"Like what?" Nick said.

"Oh, I don't know. Like the way my son pitched tonight?"

"We better start with the second inning," said Nick.

"No," his dad said. "It was the first inning that made the night special."

"You sound like Coach," Nick said.

"That's because your first pitching coach is sitting right here," Victor García said.

"And still my best."

Amelia rolled her eyes. "Could you be *more* of a kiss-up?"

Nick kicked her under the table. "Easily!"

The Garcías laughed, and it was the best sound Nick had heard all night.

The Yankees were playing again. Once the season started, they had a game practically every other day until October. By habit Nick asked Amelia if there was anything she wanted to watch on TV tonight.

"Next time, don't ask, because I *will* take you up on it."

Victor García clapped his hands together. "Let's go," he said, "before she changes her mind."

"I'll meet you in there in a sec," Nick called over his shoulder as he walked toward his bedroom. "Just gotta do one thing."

He found Amelia smirking at him from the hallway.

"The pitcher wants to write, doesn't he?" she said.

"How did you know?" Nick said.

"It's written all over your face."

It was no big secret to either friends or family how much Nick loved to write. Sometimes he thought it was the only way he felt comfortable talking about himself, revealing what was truly in his heart.

His favorite parts of English class were the writing assignments, especially the ones where he could write about a subject of his own choosing. Writing was a safe space. A release. A way for Nick to clear his brain by ejecting thoughts onto the screen of his laptop. Nick was a natural worrier, an overthinker, which could easily lead to mental exhaustion, and often did.

His dad called out from the living room that the game was in the top of the fifth. So there was a long way to go.

Nick opened his laptop and began typing with no particular plan in mind. These entries weren't like keeping a journal. He didn't build on them, or even write every day, and he often deleted them as soon as he was through. This time, he decided to write in letter format to no one special. He wrote about his dreams, for himself and Amelia, and their family. He wrote about how being afraid of so many different things had become a routine, and how wrong he thought it was for good people like his parents to suffer. Nick wrote about the unfairness and hostility his father endured for making one minor mistake in his youth, a risk he took in an effort to establish a better future for his family, even if the only family he had at the time was his wife.

Through his writing, Nick begged for just one of his prayers to be answered.

Tonight, the words flowed quickly, spilling out of him in a rush. When he was finished, or nearly finished, he reviewed what he'd written, fixing things, finding spelling mistakes, revising sentences. Nick's English teacher, Mr. Doherty, always told the class that good writing was rewriting.

"You can't take a bad pitch back," Mr. Doherty said. "But you can go back and fix a bad sentence."

He heard his dad calling him then. The Yankees were behind, 5–0, but now had a rally going. They'd cut the lead to 5–2 with the bases loaded.

"On my way," Nick yelled back.

He took one last brief look at the document on-screen before closing the laptop. Maybe, Nick thought, if he wrote stories like this often enough, he could figure out a way to write the happy ending Mrs. Gurriel was always talking about.

Before he left the room to join his dad, Nick walked over to his window and looked down at the street.

This time nobody was there staring back at him.

20

BEN SUGGESTED THAT THEY HAVE ONE OF THEIR THREE-MAN practices after lunch the next day, and told Nick to meet him at his building. They'd grab Diego on the way.

Nick felt better now after having unloaded his thoughts in writing. Lighter. Like a weight was lifted off his shoulders.

As he made the short walk to Ben's building, Nick thought about what it would be like to show Marisol his writing someday. But that would mean revealing what he'd been purposely hiding from her. His recent entries covered subjects she knew nothing about. Nick debated calling them secrets, because they weren't really. Perhaps they were just things she didn't know *yet*. Yes, that's precisely what they were. Secrets yet to be revealed to her.

Nick saw Ben up ahead now, waiting on the sidewalk in front of his building—bat over his shoulder, catcher's mitt on his left hand, Blazers cap tipped back on his head.

Nick was still a block away when he heard Ben shout, "Hey, pitcher . . . *catch!*"

Then a ball was suddenly soaring through the air, a long, accurate throw that Nick reached up easily and caught without breaking stride.

• • •

Just the sound of the ball meeting the pocket of his glove gave Nick the feeling that the best part of his day was just beginning.

"I'd like to make an announcement," Nick said after the three of them did some stretching and light throwing.

"You sound like Diego," Ben said. "But go ahead."

"I'm shutting off my brain today," Nick said, like this was a decision he'd come to after months of deliberating.

"Okay," Ben said, "but you have to be careful when you do that. Diego turned off his brain one time and obviously never remembered to turn it back on."

"You know what's funny, Kelly?" Diego said. "You trying to be funny."

After they'd all taken some batting practice, Ben hit fly balls to Nick and Diego in the outfield. Then Diego hit grounders to Nick and Ben in the infield. Finally, Nick tried his luck by telling Ben he didn't see how it could possibly hurt if he did a little pitching today, just to stretch out his arm. Ben told him to forget it; his next throw day wasn't until their game on Saturday.

"I don't know who's stricter," Nick said to Ben, "you or Coach."

"Probably a tie," Ben said.

"My arm's fine," Nick argued.

"And that's the way we plan to keep it."

"You sound like you're guarding it."

"So you noticed?"

They finished up with Nick hitting fly balls to Diego in center field, and Diego unleashing one strong throw after another to Ben at the plate. He was throwing so well today that Nick finally yelled out, "For all the talk about guarding my arm, sometimes I wonder if mine's only third-best on my own team."

"Now *that*," Diego shouted back, "is funny."

They called it a little earlier than usual today because Ben had a dentist appointment and Diego's mom wanted to take him shopping for school clothes over at the Bronx Terminal Market.

"Wait," Ben said to Diego. "School doesn't start up for another month."

Diego reached into the back pocket of his shorts and pulled out his cell phone, holding it out to Ben.

"Why don't you call my mom and tell her that," Diego said.

"I would rather take a foul ball off my mask," Ben said. "Or my fingers, for that matter."

"Thought so," Diego said.

They started walking toward 161st Street. Ben and Diego made a right turn in the direction of home, but Nick stopped and said he was going to hang around the Stadium for a while.

"The Yankees aren't playing until tonight," Ben said. "It's probably way too early for any of the players to be showing up."

"I like to walk around outside even when nothing's going on," Nick said.

"Waiting for some of those Yankee ghosts to show up?" Ben said. "Not sure the team's been over here long enough to have any good ones."

"Hey," Nick said. "Mariano Rivera pitched in this Stadium. And Derek Jeter played his last home game here."

"Well," Diego said, "if you happen to run into Jeter's ghost, tell him I said hi."

Nick checked his phone. It was two thirty in the afternoon. He had no real plan, no place he needed to be in the next hour or so. It wouldn't be accurate to say he didn't have a care in the world, even on a day like today. But at least for a little while, he'd been able to tune his brain to another channel, and that was something. It had a lot to do with being with Ben and Diego. They always knew how to put things in perspective for Nick.

He walked up the steps at Babe Ruth Plaza and then over to the left, near the newly planted trees. He strolled past the media entrance and then under the huge blue letters that said GATE 4 and kept going. He may have convinced himself he didn't have a plan, but somewhere in his subconscious, Nick knew exactly where he was going: the players' parking lot behind the Stadium, on River Avenue.

It always surprised Nick how big the Stadium really was. When you walked around the perimeter, it was the equivalent of walking three city blocks. Maybe more.

Nick was hoping some of the Yankees might show up early today. He, Ben, and Diego had been out here plenty of times before, waiting to see if one of the players would stop his car in the short driveway leading to the garage. It was a long shot, but worth a try for an autograph. They had seen it happen a few times, but were never lucky enough to get one. Even Diego, who could usually charm his way through anything, hadn't managed to score a signed ball.

But Nick had stuck a permanent marker in his back pocket this morning, and a Michael Arroyo baseball card he carried with him sometimes, thinking today might be the day.

Nick wasn't as keen on autographs as Diego was, but one from Michael Arroyo would be different. So he waited out there with a few other kids, and some men he knew were professional autograph collectors. These were the guys who only wanted players' autographs so they could go off and sell them.

A black SUV pulled up suddenly, with tinted windows, so it was impossible to see who the driver was. Could that be Michael's car? Of all the things Nick knew about Michael, the kind of car he drove was not among them. But it didn't matter, because the car was barely slowing, and before he knew it, the gate was open- ing and the SUV was gone. Then, a couple minutes later, another black SUV came up the drive. It appeared to be the same model, a Lincoln Navigator. But it, too, didn't slow before pulling into the garage.

Could Michael Arroyo have been one of the drivers? Nick wasn't sure. But he reasoned that Michael would be the kind of player who would stop, especially if he saw kids waiting for him.

Michael had been one of those kids not so long ago.

He had been me, Nick thought.

Nick didn't need an autograph on a baseball card to have the kind of connection he felt with Michael Arroyo. In his heart, that bond was already as strong as it could possibly be, because of baseball, because of pitching, because of the Bronx, because of the Yankees. He didn't need Michael's signature on all that. All he needed was to remember that if Michael could overcome his obstacles, then so could Nick. Michael had made it here, to Yankee Stadium, first from Cuba and then from the Bronx, despite everything that stood in his way. Nick wanted to believe that seeing Michael Arroyo pitch was like getting a glimpse of his own future.

He started walking home, bat over his shoulder, glove hanging from it, permanent marker jammed in his pocket along with the unsigned baseball card. All in all, it had been a pretty good day. Maybe he would text Marisol when he got home and see if she wanted to hang out. That would make a good day even better.

He walked past Joyce Kilmer Park, where he and Ben and Diego would play catch when all the fields were taken at Macombs Dam Park. It was a beautiful park that stretched for blocks on the other side of the Grand Concourse across from Nick's building.

Briefly glancing up from the sidewalk, Nick stopped dead in his tracks. He had to be hallucinating.

It couldn't be, but yet there he was, plain as day, standing at one of the park gates.

The ICE Man, handing out flyers to people walking in and out of the park, smiling, and looking as friendly as could be.

Nick knew better.

But when he turned to run this time, the ICE Man ran after him.

21

"WAIT!" THE ICE MAN SAID.

Nick ran as fast as his legs would carry him. Not sure where, just back in the direction from which he'd come.

"Hey!" The man was yelling now. "Hey . . . stop!"

Nick looked back over his shoulder. The man was short of breath and slowing his pace, but smiling nonetheless.

"C'mon," the man called out again. "I just want to talk to you. You're the one carrying a baseball bat."

Nick stopped running, against his better judgment, his hackles up, ready to dodge if the situation escalated.

As the ICE Man approached, Nick bristled and said sharply, "I'm not supposed to talk to strangers, least of all *you*."

They were just a few feet apart now. The man clutched the stack of flyers in his hand, but Nick couldn't tell what they were for.

"Who do you think I am?" the man asked, breathing hard from the run.

"Why were you watching my game the other day?" Nick said instead.

"That's not an answer."

"Neither is that," Nick said pointedly.

"Okay," the man said, realizing he was the adult here. "I'll go first. I like baseball and stopped to watch on my way home from work."

"I saw you taking notes," Nick said.

The ICE Man was standing right in front of him now on the street.

I shouldn't be talking to this guy.

But there was something about this man—Nick couldn't put his finger on it. He'd been afraid of him for so long, but for some unknown reason, he didn't feel that way now.

"The notes? That was just work stuff. When I remember things, I write them down before I can forget. It's why I always carry a small notebook with me," he said, pulling said notebook out of his back pocket. "Sometimes things make more sense to me when I write them down."

Nick was compelled to tell the man he was the exact same way, but held his tongue. He wasn't looking to make a new friend.

"Now it's your turn," the man said. "Who do you think I am? And why did you run?"

"That's two questions," Nick said.

The man grinned. "Neither one of them is much of a brain buster."

"You're with ICE," Nick said, with an accusatory glare. "I saw you and your guys raid that house across the street the other night."

The man's eyes were saucers, and he startled Nick right then by letting out a hearty laugh.

"I don't know who you thought you saw at that raid the other night," the man said, "but it wasn't me."

He handed Nick one of the flyers in his hand.

At the top, in big letters, it read, "ICE Home Arrests. Protect Your Rights."

Nick looked down at the flyer and realized his hand was shaking. "I don't understand," he said.

"Then let me explain, kid," the man said. "I'm one of the good guys."

His name was Ryan Gasson, and he was an immigration lawyer. He had an office on 161st Street and worked for a law firm called the Bronx Defenders.

Nick looked around.

"I still probably shouldn't be talking to you," he said.

"Let me guess—you've probably seen me outside your building before, right?" Mr. Gasson said.

"How would you even know that?" Nick said.

Mr. Gasson smiled again.

"I know a lot about this neighborhood," he said. "I grew up on 170th."

"Why are you handing these out?" Nick said, holding up the flyer.

"We call them 'KYR' pamphlets," Mr. Gasson explained. "'Know Your Rights.' There's a lot of important information in them, especially about what to do if ICE tries to enter a home illegally."

"Illegally how?" Nick said.

"Without a signed warrant from a judge," Mr. Gasson replied.

"I didn't know they needed that."

"You'd be surprised how many people don't," Mr. Gasson said. "Including adults. *Especially* adults."

They were walking back in the direction of Nick's building now, but Nick knew not to stop in front of it. No matter how good this guy claimed to be, he was still a stranger. And Nick didn't want him knowing his home address.

"I still can't believe it," Nick said.

"Believe what?"

"You look so much like the man I saw leading the ICE raid," Nick said. "I was sure he was you. And you were him."

"Except he wants to send people out of the country and I work to keep them here," Mr. Gasson said. "I've been all over the Bronx, but focusing on this neighborhood for the last couple of weeks, trying to quietly find out who might need our help."

He knows I live in the area, Nick thought. *What else does he know about me? Or my dad?* Suddenly Nick recalled the advice from Ben's father: know when to keep your mouth shut.

Just because he seemed nice and had these flyers didn't mean that Nick could trust him. It could be a scam or a hoax.

"You must know some families that are worried about ICE," Mr. Gasson said.

"No," Nick said, too quickly.

It was a lie, of course, and he wondered if Mr. Gasson sensed it.

Then Mr. Gasson reached into his back pocket, pulled out his wallet, and took out a business card with THE BRONX DEFENDERS in raised print across the center.

"That's got my office number on it," Mr. Gasson said. Then he patted his jacket and shirt pocket, but shook his head.

"This is a dumb question, but you don't happen to have a pen on you, do you?"

Nick reached into his own back pocket and came out with the marker he'd hoped to hand to Michael Arroyo.

Mr. Gasson thanked him, turned the card over, and scribbled something down. "That's my cell number," he said. "Hold on to that card. If you ever know somebody who might need my help, they can call that number any time of the day or night."

Nick took it, and slid the card into his back pocket behind his Michael Arroyo card. Then Mr. Gasson handed him a couple more flyers. Nick read all the way through to the bottom of the page. In big block letters at the top were the questions "What can I do if ICE officers are at my door?" and "Do I have to let ICE into my home?"

Nick was surprised to find that the answer was no, at least not if they didn't have the warrant Mr. Gasson had mentioned. Farther down the page, it explained what to say if the ICE agents didn't have a warrant. You were supposed to tell them that they didn't have your consent, and you had the right to tell them to leave.

Nick wondered if that would actually work, if they would care to listen to anything you said once they were inside.

He kept reading. "What should I do if ICE agents are already inside my home?"

Nick didn't think there was anything you *could* do.

The answer was to tell them right away if there was an elderly person present. Or someone who was ill and on medication.

Like Amelia, Nick thought.

The last question on the flyer was the part Nick didn't want to think about: what to do if a loved one *was* arrested by ICE.

He took a deep breath, let it out, the way he did when he was trying to relax himself on the mound.

"I'll pass these around," Nick said.

"You'll be doing a good thing," Mr. Gasson said.

By now they were walking past Nick's building, but Nick made sure not to stop.

"Can I ask one more question?" Mr. Gasson said.

"I really need to get going," Nick said, a little impatient.

"It's one I already asked," Mr. Gasson said. "Why did you turn and run when you saw me?"

"I told you that already," Nick said. "You looked like the man at the raid. From ICE."

"But why are *you* afraid of ICE?" Mr. Gasson said in a quiet voice.

Nick inwardly kicked himself for being so obvious, but then, maybe he was just paranoid.

"Because ICE isn't nice," he said simply.

Mr. Gasson smiled again. "Don't lose that card."

Then he stepped off the sidewalk and crossed the street toward the park.

He knows, Nick told himself, sounding out of breath even inside his own head. *I don't know how. But he does.*

22 ⚾⚾⚾⚾⚾⚾⚾⚾⚾⚾⚾⚾⚾⚾⚾

AMELIA WAS ON THE COUCH READING. THE BOOK SAID *TO KILL A Mockingbird* in big cursive letters at the top, by an author named Harper Lee.

"Summer reading?" Nick asked.

Amelia didn't even glance up from the page. "Well, it's summer, and I'm reading. But it's not on my required reading list, if that's what you're asking."

Then she looked up from the book and studied Nick's face. "You look like you saw a ghost," she said.

"Everybody wants to talk about ghosts lately," Nick said, hanging his Blazers cap on the hook by the door.

Neither of their parents was home yet, so Nick took the opportunity to tell Amelia about his run-in with Mr. Gasson. She was relieved to hear that he wasn't the ICE Man after all.

Nick handed Amelia one of the flyers, and she read through it quickly, nodding her head as she did.

"You think he was telling the truth?" Nick asked his sister.

"If he's not, I don't know why he'd waste his time handing out these flyers," she said.

"I think he must be hanging around our neighborhood because so many people don't seem to know the facts," Nick said.

"Maybe Dad should talk to Mr. Gasson," Amelia said. "He's always worried about the law. Who better to talk to than an immigration lawyer?"

They sat there in silence for a couple of minutes, Nick in the armchair across from Amelia, a small coffee table between them covered in flyers.

"Are you okay now?" Amelia said finally.

Nick grinned. "Yeah, I think so. It was just so strange. Took a while for my brain to separate the ICE Man from Mr. Gasson."

Amelia nodded.

Another silence filled the room before Nick broke it. "Do you think our prayers really will be answered one of these days?"

"A hundred percent," she said.

"You sound as sure as Mrs. Gurriel."

Amelia laughed. "No one could be *that* sure."

"You really mean it, don't you?" Nick said.

"I wouldn't say it if I didn't believe it," she said. "I'm even trying to figure out a way to fire up a prayer of my own."

"Oh yeah? How?"

"You know I can't say," she said. "You're the one who's always so superstitious about saying your dreams aloud."

"Good point."

"But I'll make you a deal," she said. "If this one does come through, I promise, you'll be the first to know."

"Deal," Nick said.

Amelia picked up her book again, and Nick went to go put his stuff away in his room. But when he got there, he saw the laptop open on his desk and felt an overwhelming desire to write.

Nick wasn't sure if meeting Mr. Gasson qualified as a happy ending. But finding out he wasn't the ICE Man would certainly do for now.

23

THEY HELD A FAMILY MEETING IN THE KITCHEN AFTER VICTOR AND Graciela García returned home from work to discuss Nick's encounter with Mr. Gasson.

One of the flyers was lying faceup on the table, along with Mr. Gasson's card, the one with his cell phone number on the back.

Nick's dad peered at them skeptically, then pushed them to the middle of the table.

"He cannot help me and he cannot help us," he said decisively.

Nick started to contest, but Amelia beat him to it.

"Daddy," she said, "you don't know that."

She called him "Daddy" when she wanted him to see her as his little girl. Mostly, so she could get him to come around to her side.

"I know what I know," Victor García said.

"But how do you know this lawyer can't help us if you don't even talk to him?" Amelia said, trying to break through her father's stubbornness.

"We have spoken to lawyers in the past," their mom said calmly. "The last one said that if your father even attempted to contact the government, he could open himself up to arrest and deportation."

Nick wasn't ready to give up just yet. "But Mr. Gasson sounded like he really wants to help people like us," he insisted, "and to defend our rights, like it says on his card: 'The Bronx Defenders.'"

His dad slowly turned his chair to face Nick.

"We cannot afford lawyers even if I wanted one," he said.

At times, Nick couldn't tell where his dad's strength ended and his stubbornness began. But he knew that when he made up his mind, it was as if his decision were set in cement.

"But, Daddy," Amelia said, "how can you know how much this Mr. Gasson might cost if you don't even ask him? If he's handing out these flyers on the street, maybe he isn't looking for money. Maybe he's just looking for people to help."

Their dad slapped the table with his hand. He didn't look angry, Nick thought. Just tired.

"We cannot trust anybody outside this room," he said.

"What about my friends?" Nick asked.

"Sometimes I wish you hadn't told them as much as you have," Victor García said.

Nick's heart sank down to his stomach. He knew Ben and Diego would never tell anybody or betray his trust. But it hurt to think he'd in some way disobeyed his father by exposing their family's secrets. Even to the two people he considered brothers.

Victor García leaned back in his chair and closed his eyes. Nick knew by now that his father always looked tired when he got home from work, but there was something different tonight. His dad almost seemed defeated, even though Nick felt terrible thinking it. In Nick's heart, his dad was his real hero, more than any baseball player could ever be. His dad had *always* been his hero.

Nick's mom said nothing, just looked across the table at her husband.

But Amelia wasn't giving up.

"When did you talk to the last lawyer?" she asked.

Nick's dad massaged his temples. "I don't know," he said. "Two years ago. Maybe three."

"But see, Daddy, that's the thing," she said. "So much has changed in the past few years."

"Yes, things have changed," their dad said. "For the worse."

"We can't give up hope," Nick said. "You and Mom are always telling us that."

His dad turned to him again. "But I don't want false hope, either, son. To me that's almost more cruel than no hope at all."

He pushed back from the table now, his chair loudly scraping the floor. Then, one by one, Victor García leaned down and kissed each of his children on the top of their head before exiting the kitchen. Their mom followed.

"It's like being sick and refusing to call a doctor," Amelia whispered to Nick when they were out of earshot.

"I *know*," he said, keeping his own voice low.

"Maybe Mom can talk some sense into him," Amelia said. "She's as stubborn as he is."

Nick grinned. "Don't let her hear you say that."

"I don't know why he thinks talking to Mr. Gasson would be showing weakness," Amelia said.

"We have to find a way to change his mind," Nick said.

"Or at least try."

"I thought we just did."

Amelia said, "We have to try harder."

She got up and went to her room then, and Nick went to his. When he turned on his radio, the Yankee game was in the eighth inning, and the score was tied, 4–4. But as much as he wanted the Yankees to win every single game, tonight he hoped they'd go into extra innings. He wanted to be in his bed listening to baseball until he fell asleep.

He wanted baseball to be the last thing he heard tonight.

Only it wasn't.

The game was still tied in the ninth when his door creaked open, revealing Nick's dad standing in the light from the hallway.

"I just want you to know how much I love you," Victor García said. "And how much your mother and I appreciate you finding that lawyer."

"More like he found me," Nick said.

His dad said nothing for a moment. The only voice in the room was John Sterling's, announcing that the Yankees had their leadoff man on first. Nick turned down the volume.

"I don't want you passing out flyers," his dad said. "All that will do is direct attention to you, and perhaps me." He paused. "Okay?"

It wasn't really a question.

"Okay," Nick confirmed.

"I mean it, Nicolás."

"Nicolás" meant business. Solidified their agreement.

"And I don't want you talking to that lawyer again if you see him in the neighborhood," Victor García said. "Whatever help you think he can offer will only hurt us by drawing attention to our family."

"You know best," Nick said, even though he believed the opposite was true tonight.

"This is what I want," his dad said, and walked out of the room. In the very next moment, Nick could hear John Sterling's voice rising, shouting about a ball "rolling all the way to the wall!"

The winning run for the Yankees was crossing home plate, and John Sterling shouted, "The Yankees win . . . Thuhhhhhhhhhhh . . . Yankees . . . *win!*"

Nick should have been excited, but he couldn't seem to muster the joy he usually felt from a Yankee win. Instead, he got out of bed and walked down the hall to the kitchen. Flicking on the light, Nick could see the flyer and Mr. Gasson's card on the table, right where his father had left them. Nick picked them up and brought them into his room, where he placed them both in the bottom drawer of his desk. But first, he punched Mr. Gasson's number into his phone and hit save.

The Bronx Defenders.

It sounded like a baseball team.

One his dad thought was out of their league.

24

MARISOL TEXTED NICK THAT SHE WAS GOING TO BE AWAY FOR A FEW days. There was a gap in her league schedule, so she was going up to New Haven, Connecticut, with some of the girls on her team to play in a weekend tournament.

Show them what you got, Nick texted back.

Gotta get my Serena vibe going, she wrote back.

While Marisol had her two-day tournament this weekend, the Blazers had another game, which was supposed to be Nick's second-to-last start before the championship. If they made it there. Except Coach Viera had hinted that if the Blazers locked up their spot in the big game, he might hold Nick out of his last regularly scheduled start.

Nick didn't like the sound of that. Not at all. He and Coach were discussing it before Nick went to warm up with Ben.

"I just want to pitch as much as I possibly can," Nick said to Coach Viera.

They were leaning against the fence. Out in the distance was a sign featuring another old quote from Satchel Paige: "Sometimes you win, sometimes you lose, sometimes you get rained out."

"You'd pitch all of our games if I let you," Coach said. "Then at the end of the tournament I could tell people how I blew out the arm of a future Michael Arroyo by overusing him."

"But you're not overusing me!" Nick said. "The way the schedule works out, I'd have plenty of rest before the championship."

"But think of how strong your arm would be with even *more* rest," Coach countered.

"How often do you hear about pitchers who've had *too* much time off and performed *too* well because of it?" Nick asked, attempting to back Coach into a corner. "And who's always telling me that pitchers are creatures of routine?"

"Who's always telling *me* that we shouldn't get ahead of ourselves?" Coach Viera said.

Nick grinned. *Touché.* But it wasn't over yet.

"Don't managers in the big leagues set their pitching rotations a month in advance sometimes?" Nick said.

"I give up," Coach said, throwing up his hands. "Sometimes when we have these little debates, it's like trying to get a hit off you."

"Grab a bat," Nick said.

"No thank you."

The Orioles already had two losses. If they wanted to give themselves any shot at making the championship game, they had to beat Nick and the Blazers tonight.

"This is like a playoff game for them," Diego stated before the Blazers were set to take the field for the top of the first. They were the home team tonight.

"So what?" Ben said. "Every game is like the playoffs for us."

"The Orioles still have to play like there's no tomorrow."

"You always hear that," Ben said. "But if they lose, does that mean they have to skip Sunday?"

Diego frowned. "Don't play your mind games with me."

"Wouldn't be much of a game," Ben said.

The three of them sat together on the bench, Ben in the middle. He stretched out his hand, and Nick and Diego put theirs on top. It was one of those small moments that reminded Nick of how big their friendship was. Bigger than the tournament, even bigger than baseball.

It was time to take the mound then. Nick and Diego ran onto the field together, and Ben took his spot behind home. Now all Nick needed to do was find out how much life he had in his fastball tonight.

A lot, as it turned out.

He struck out the side in the top of the first, on eleven pitches. Then he struck out the first two batters in the second before the sixth guy in the Orioles' order, their catcher, managed to bloop a single over Ronnie Lester at second and into short right field on what the announcers call an "excuse-me swing."

The catcher, Harold Rosario, had been lucky to get a piece of the ball. Nick gave Ben a shrug and a *so what?* look and struck out the next guy on three pitches. Good morning, good afternoon, good night. This wasn't just going to be a good night. It was going to be a great one. Seven batters so far, six strikeouts.

Let's do this.

The Blazers were already ahead, 2–0, because Ben hit a two-runner home in the bottom of the first. The ball had rolled all the way to the infield on the adjoining field closest to River Avenue.

Nick's mom was here tonight with Amelia. His dad had to

work late at the restaurant, which was busiest on Saturday nights. Sometimes, he wouldn't come home until well after midnight. Marisol was playing the final round of her tournament in New Haven tomorrow, bringing her own kind of heat up there.

Nick was bringing his.

He was throwing his best fastball of the whole tournament. Broadcasters would occasionally talk about pitchers having an extra yard on their fastballs. Nick was experiencing that tonight. Every once in a while, Ben would mix in a changeup, just for the fun of it—to freeze a hitter, or get him swinging wildly before the ball even reached the plate.

But mostly it was the pitch Ben had taken to calling "number one." Heat and more heat. Nick knew his pitch count was decent, because of all the strikeouts. Maybe this was the night he could talk Coach into letting him finish what he'd started.

After he struck out two more guys in the top of the fourth, Ben mimicked Coach. "We having any fun yet?"

They were ahead 5–0 by then.

"Maybe we should save some of this good stuff for another day," Ben said.

Nick looked at him as if he couldn't believe what he'd just heard. "You're kidding, right?"

"I never kid about your arm."

Nick wished Ben didn't have to be so practical all the time.

"Well, you *must* be kidding if you think I'm asking out of this game."

"Nick's right," Diego said to Ben. They were sitting on the bench with their water bottles out. "Say you've got three hits in a game, with a chance to go four-for-four your last time up. Would you ask Coach to take you out so you could save your swing?"

"Not the same thing," Ben said.

"But it kind of is," Diego pressed. "When you're going good, you wanna keep going. When a shooter gets hot in basketball, he wants to keep shooting."

Ben was quiet for a moment and then said, "You know what I hate?"

"What?" Diego said.

"When you're right."

Diego beamed and high-fived Nick. "Man," he said, "that has *got* to sting!"

Before they went back out for the top of the fifth, Coach informed Nick it would be his last inning.

"But I haven't thrown that many pitches, Coach," Nick said. "I checked the book."

"And after you throw a few more, you're coming out of the game, and we all go home happy," Coach Viera said. "Except maybe the Orioles."

"No, think about it, Coach," Diego said. "Even the Orioles will be happy."

"How do you figure?"

"Because Nick will be out of the game!"

Diego turned to Ben, put up his hand for a high five. "I'm on a roll," he said.

By the time Nick was back on the mound, the Blazers' lead was 7–0.

He struck out the Orioles' third baseman to start the fifth, making it ten strikeouts for the game. He didn't typically check the book for his strikeout total, but tonight he had. Ten was the most he'd had the whole tournament. Two batters to go if he wanted to beat that and get to eleven. Two more chances. His pitch count was sixty-eight coming into the inning, well short of eighty.

The next batter was Benny Alvarez, the Orioles' first baseman. Possibly the biggest kid in the Dream League, Benny was a left-handed hitter with a ton of power who led the league in home runs. Nick thought he had a pretty good shot at MVP.

But Benny hadn't hit any home runs tonight, because Nick had struck him out twice already.

And it looked as if Nick might do it a third time, getting ahead of him oh-and-two. Ben set up on the inside corner then, since they'd struck out Benny his first two times up with inside fastballs.

Nick took a deep breath. This was the fun part. Trying to finish a hitter off.

He nodded at Ben, went into his motion, and put the ball exactly where he wanted it. Benny took a huge swing, but only managed to tip the ball off the handle, hitting a slow roller up the first baseline.

Very slow.

Head down, Benny busted out of the box, thinking he might get himself an infield hit, at least something to show for his night at the plate.

Nick broke off the mound, knowing he had to book it himself, because Benny was fast.

He could see the play in his head as he closed on the ball. See himself reaching down, barehanding the ball, sidearming it to Darryl in one smooth motion.

All of which he did.

Small problem: Big Benny Alvarez.

As Nick bent down to swipe the ball, Benny sprinted head-first, trying to leg out a hit.

And went crashing into Nick just as he released the ball, sending him helicoptering through the air.

When Nick came down in the grass between the first baseline and the mound, he landed on his shoulder.

His right shoulder.

His pitching shoulder.

Landed hard.

25

BEN GOT TO NICK FIRST, BARELY BEATING COACH VIERA.

Rolled over onto his back, Nick lay, knees up, with his feet flat on the turf, cradling his arm. He'd gotten the wind knocked out of him from landing the way he did, unable to break his fall. It was as if he got sucker punched by the ground.

But that wasn't what had him worried. He knew he would be breathing normally in a minute.

Nick wanted the pain behind his shoulder to go away. It hurt back there, a lot. But he wasn't going to admit that out loud right now.

Somehow Diego had made it over from center field already, and was standing over Nick, beside Ben. So were the Blazers' infielders. The home-plate umpire stood behind Coach Viera, who was kneeling next to Nick.

Nick faked a smile, and in a weak voice said, "I'm okay."

"Can you sit up?" Coach asked, a hand placed gently on Nick's shoulder.

"Sure, no probs," Nick said.

Ben reached down to help, and Nick used his left hand to grab Ben's, not wanting to cause any further damage to his shoulder.

He didn't say anything, but Nick could see that Ben had noticed. Ben never missed a thing, at least not where Nick was concerned.

"That's what I get for trying to learn to fly in the middle of a ball game," Nick said, trying to do his part to lighten the mood. And the tension.

"It looked to me like you landed pretty good on your right side," Coach said. Nick sensed a hint of alarm in his voice.

"Felt like I landed on my whole body at once."

Diego, being Diego, tried to lighten the mood, even though Nick could see the concern on his face.

"Like they say in the Olympics," he said, "at least you stuck the landing."

Nick resisted the impulse to rub his shoulder. There was an old expression in baseball about how batters weren't supposed to rub the spot where they'd just gotten hit by a pitch. The idea was not to let the other guy know it hurt.

Nick wasn't going to let anybody know, at least not for the time being.

Now up in a sitting position, he could see his mom and Amelia had come down from the bleachers and were standing up against the fence behind first base. They were trying not to interfere in the game, but were listening in to make sure it wasn't anything serious.

"Your arm okay?" Diego asked.

"Perfect," Nick said.

Nick insisted he could stand up by himself. Ben picked up his glove and Diego grabbed Nick's hat, which had gone flying off during the fall. The fans in the bleachers applauded. So did the Blazers and the Orioles.

Nick grabbed his gear from Ben and Diego and started walking in the direction of the mound. Coach caught up with him and gently put a hand on Nick's arm, wordlessly guiding him in the direction of the Blazers' bench.

As they got to the baseline, Nick called over to Darryl at first base.

"Did we get the out?"

"Got Benny by a step," Darryl said.

When Nick was sitting on the bench, Benny came over to him, red in the face.

"Dude," he said, "I am *so* sorry."

Nick put out his fist so Benny could tap it with his own.

"We were both just trying to make a play," Nick said. "No worries."

Yeah, right, Nick thought. *No worries?*

Darryl's mom, who came to every game, volunteered as an emergency medical technician. She was mostly concerned about Nick's ribs. But when she pressed down on the area, Nick told her he didn't feel any pain. Then she asked him, just to be on the safe side, to lift his right arm over his head. When he did, the pain wasn't as severe as he'd expected.

But the pain was there nonetheless. The best thing would be to start icing it now, but asking for an ice pack would be the same as announcing to everybody that something was wrong. So he would power through until the end of the game, and figure out a way to ice his shoulder when he got home.

One more secret.

After Darryl's mom finished examining him, Nick and Ben sat down together on the end of the bench. Ben had made the last out of the previous inning, which meant he wouldn't be hitting this time unless the Blazers batted around. So there was no need for him to remove his catcher's gear.

Staring straight ahead, he said in a soft voice, "How bad?"

"Not as bad as I thought when I landed," Nick said.

"Nick . . ."

"It hurts behind my shoulder. Like somebody whacked it with a bat."

"What are you gonna do?"

"Get some ice on it when I get home and hope it feels better," Nick said, as if to say, *What else can I do?*

"Maybe you need a doctor."

"Doctor" was like a four-letter word, to be avoided at all costs. He thought of how hard it was to find the right health center when Amelia was sick; he didn't want to be a burden on his family.

"If I see a doctor, that means I'm really hurt," Nick said.

"And you can't be hurt."

Nick could feel some tears coming, but squeezed them back. No crying in baseball.

"I *know*," Nick said.

"This was your best game."

Nick sighed. "Yeah."

"This isn't fair," Ben said.

"What is anymore?"

On the walk home after the Blazers' 8–2 victory, Nick's mom kept chattering on about what a fright he'd given her. Nick promised her the next time he tried a belly flop, he'd make sure it was in a swimming pool.

"Are you sure you're not hurt?" Graciela García asked, neurotic mother kicking in.

"Sore," Nick said. "Not hurt. There's a difference."

"Sore where?"

"Everywhere!"

He knew he would have to tell Amelia the truth when they got home. He'd need an accomplice to help him with the ice and, of course, to keep their mom from finding out. Nick's mom had plenty to worry about. He didn't want to add to the pile.

As soon as they were inside the apartment, Graciela asked if Nick was hungry. She thought food could cure just about anything. But Nick said he wasn't, and just wanted to relax and listen to the Yankees on the radio.

"Me too," Amelia said, following Nick to his room.

"Wait, *you* want to listen to baseball?" Graciela García asked, suspicious.

"What?" Amelia said. "I can't like baseball?"

Graciela gave her a look. "Well, enjoy," she said. "I'll be in my room reading if you need me."

As soon as they were in Nick's room, Amelia closed the door and said, "What is it?"

"Was I that obvious?"

"You were even carrying your arm funny on the way home," she said. "Mom didn't notice because she was blabbing away like she always does when she's nervous."

"I think I did something to my shoulder," Nick said, finally allowing himself to rub it, "and need to get some ice on it."

Without another word, Amelia left the room, and came back a couple minutes later with a plastic sandwich bag full of ice.

"Did Mom hear you?" Nick asked.

"I told her I was getting an iced tea."

Then she asked if she could look at his shoulder. Nick took off his jersey and sat on his bed while Amelia surveyed the damage. "There's a bruise forming back there, but not a big one."

Nick pulled his Bronx Bombers T-shirt out of his dresser drawer and put it on, placing the ice bag over his shoulder. Before he could lie down, Amelia asked him to imitate his pitching motion so she could check his range.

Nick couldn't help it; he laughed at how seriously she was taking all this.

"I know you spend a lot of time with doctors," he said, "but now you think you are one?"

Nick stood near the head of his bed, next to the Michael Arroyo poster. He stepped toward his sister with his left foot and brought his arm up and forward.

It still hurt.

But didn't kill.

"So?" Amelia said.

"Not excruciating," Nick said.

"So now we ice," she said.

Ice, Nick thought.

Tonight, it was his friend.

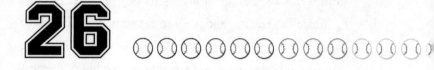
A FEW HOURS LATER, NICK WAS JOLTED AWAKE BY THE SOUND OF HIS father's keys in the front door. Nick still had the ice pack. He got up, muscles screaming, and tiptoed quietly down the hall to the bathroom, where he emptied the bag of ice-turned-water into the sink.

He heard his parents murmuring in Spanish in the kitchen, and could only assume his mom was filling his dad in about Nick's collision with Big Benny Alvarez.

Nick was shuffling back to his room, when his father intercepted him.

"How are you?"

"I'm okay."

"I thought we had agreed you would avoid contact sports," he joked.

"Tell that to Benny Alvarez. He contacted me before I contacted the ground."

"I gotta keep you in one piece so you can make it all the way to the big leagues," his dad said.

"Don't worry," Nick said. "I'm like you. Built to last."

"You'll feel better in the morning," his dad said, giving him a pat on the shoulder. Mercifully, the left one.

Nick got back into bed. His shoulder still ached, but not the way it had on the field. Lying on his left side seemed to help. He thought about sneaking some more ice after his dad went to bed, but decided against it. It wasn't worth getting caught.

He wedged a pillow next to him so he wouldn't roll over onto his right side during the night, and let his eyes droop closed.

In the gap between awake and sleep, Nick hit the instant-replay button on tonight's encounter. The moment he came crashing down on his pitching shoulder, he'd actually thought his season might be over.

For now, though, he was still in the tournament.

Still in the game.

The area behind his shoulder was stiff and sore in the morning, but didn't feel any worse than last night. Or was that just Nick brushing it off, when he might have a serious injury? To check, he stood up carefully and brought his right arm behind him, lifting it over his head and bringing it forward.

His shoulder growled, but didn't bark. Or howl. That was a good sign.

He resolved to take a day off from baseball to rest his arm and maybe ice it a bit more once he had the apartment to himself. His dad was working the lunch shift at the restaurant, and his mom was cleaning two apartments today, filling in for a housekeeper friend who came down with the flu. Amelia was at her friend's apartment on Gerard Avenue.

Before Graciela García left that morning, she told Nick that Mrs. Gurriel would be around all day, in case he needed anything.

Before she left, Nick asked Amelia if it was possible to over-ice an injury. "Impossible," she'd said. He didn't know how she knew, but he trusted her judgment. So after everyone left for the day, Nick got back in bed, laid the ice behind him, and read a book his mom brought home from the library, about a boy who got to be a batboy for the Detroit Tigers one summer.

He'd already texted Ben and Diego to let them know he was feeling better. They asked if he wanted to hang out, but he said he was going to try to take it easy and chill. Hard not to be chill when you had an ice bag permanently attached to your shoulder.

After he'd fixed himself a peanut butter and jelly sandwich for lunch, a triple-decker, he decided to go down and visit Mrs. Gurriel.

She had a way of making him feel better about almost everything.

When she opened the door and saw it was Nick standing there, her face lit up.

"To what do I owe this great pleasure?" she said grandly, like she was welcoming him into Buckingham Palace.

"I haven't seen you in a few days," Nick said.

"What's wrong?" she said, her face instantly awash with worry.

"Does something have to be wrong for me to come visit my honorary grandmother?"

"No, it does not *have* to be," she said. "But something is, Nicolás. So why don't you come in and tell me about it."

She sat at one end of her plush pink couch, and Nick sat at the other. Mrs. Gurriel had lots of little trinkets and old picture frames adorning her apartment. It was like walking into a museum, and Nick was careful not to touch anything. She asked if he'd like something to eat or drink, but he politely declined. From somewhere in her apartment Nick could hear what he knew by now was opera music. Mrs. Gurriel loved the opera. She once told him it was the music she expected to hear in heaven someday.

"So," she said, "what's going on in your beautiful life?"

Nick shifted uncomfortably in his seat. "Not always so beautiful," he said.

"I am referring to the beauty you carry around inside you, Nicolás."

He told her what happened. She listened without interrupting, nodding occasionally, her face solemn.

"Uh-huh," she said after he'd finished. "How soon were you able to apply ice to your shoulder after it happened?"

"Not until I got home," he said. "Didn't want to stress out Mom."

"Of course," Mrs. G said, giving Nick a knowing smile. "Mind if I take a look? See where the problem is?"

"Be my guest," Nick said.

She told him to turn around so his back was facing her. She moved over on the couch and proceeded to press her fingers into various spots behind Nick's shoulder.

"Tell me when it hurts," she said.

"There," Nick said when she got to a muscle near the top of the shoulder.

"Just as I thought."

"What is it?"

"The deltoid muscle," she said.

"What does that mean?" Nick asked, his nerves getting the better of him.

"It means you'll likely be fine," she said. "It would be bad if you tore it, but I don't think you did."

"You can tell all that just by poking around back there?"

"Before I became a nurse in the states, I worked as a sobadora in Mexico," she said. "A massage therapist. I can see more with my hands than my aging eyes these days."

She asked Nick to call his mom and assure her that everything was fine, but he was a little stiff and Mrs. Gurriel thought a deep-tissue massage might be the best thing for him.

"But I don't want her to worry," Nick said, still uncertain that telling his mom was the best idea.

"She won't once I talk to her," Mrs. G said. "But I would never work on you, not for one second, without her permission."

As soon as Graciela answered, she asked Nick if he was all right. He said he was, and that Mrs. G wanted to talk to her. Mrs. G spoke quickly in Spanish to Nick's mom, smiling the whole time until she ended the call.

"So," she said, clapping her hands together, "let us get to work."

"And this is going to make my shoulder feel better?"

"Well," Mrs. G said, "maybe not at first."

"This is going to hurt, isn't it?" Nick said.

"What do you boys say?" she said. "No pain, no gain."

Nick lay on his stomach and Mrs. G knelt next to the couch. She wasn't kidding. It did hurt at first, not that he would let her on to that. He was amazed at how strong her hands were as she worked both shoulders and the middle of his back. Curiously, she spent very little time on his deltoid muscle.

As she worked, she explained to Nick that the last doctor she worked with taught her something called active release technique.

"It's abbreviated as ART."

"Like actual art?" Nick asked.

"The doctor said it is if you do it right."

"So you help the injured muscle by working *other* muscles?"

"That's the idea."

She worked on him for a while, and eventually the pressure from the massage started to hurt less. The opera music played soothingly in the background. Nick could feel himself drooling on one of Mrs. Gurriel's couch cushions, his eyes fluttering shut, when finally he heard her say, "All done."

Nick groggily pushed himself up, and Mrs. Gurriel had him raise his arm, ordering him to move it back and forth.

He did.

"And?" she asked expectantly.

A wide smile formed on Nick's face.

"It doesn't hurt!" he said.

"Good," she said. "If I had thought you'd done any real damage, I would have referred you to a doctor I know near the Stadium who deals with athletic injuries. But based on my professional opinion, I didn't believe you did, and the proof is standing right in front of me."

"What's it going to feel like when it's time for me to pitch again?"

"Why don't we find out?"

"Where?"

"Right here," she said, "at Gurriel Field."

She held up a finger for Nick to wait, and scurried into her kitchen. She came back a few minutes later, proudly holding up what roughly resembled a baseball.

"I made it out of Bounty paper towel and some packing tape," she said, casually tossing the ball to Nick.

Then the elderly woman with the white hair shifted the chair closest to the couch out of the way and moved back near the door to the kitchen. She motioned for Nick to back up toward the front door.

"You're going to catch?" Nick said, skeptical.

"You think I can't?"

"Are you sure you want to do this?"

"Just pitch," she said, picking up a pillow from the couch and walking it over to the kitchen, dropping it on the floor in front of her.

"Home plate," she said.

Then she got into a catcher's crouch, and Nick couldn't help but be impressed.

Then the two of them played catch. Nick didn't go into a full windup, but made sure to simulate his pitching motion.

He threw softly.

But he threw without pain.

"How does it feel?" Mrs. G said after a few throws.

"Good?"

"Was that a question?"

"I feel great," Nick corrected.

Nick threw a few more, with the opera music cheering him on from the other room.

Finally Mrs. G said, "Okay, last one. And bring the heat. That's what they say, right?"

"That's what they say," Nick affirmed.

And that's what he did, throwing a perfect strike across an apartment that, funny enough, seemed to be full of baseball today.

Baseball and the magic of Mrs. G.

27

NICK'S MOM SPOKE AGAIN WITH MRS. GURRIEL WHEN SHE GOT home from work, and Mrs. G said Nick had suffered a slight bruise to his shoulder muscle, nothing more. And that she treated it the same way she would have done a back spasm.

"I would never do anything to jeopardize Nicolás's right arm," Mrs. G told Nick's mom. "I know how valuable it is."

"She said that?" Nick asked his mom later.

"Her exact words."

"What she did for my shoulder today feels like an answered prayer."

"May it be the first of many."

Nick told his mom that since his shoulder was feeling better, there was no point in telling his dad about it. But Graciela reminded him that while his father was adamant about keeping family secrets from the world, he didn't much like when family secrets were kept from him.

"Technically," Nick said, "it would only be a secret if I was still in pain, which I'm not."

"If it starts to hurt again, you promise you'll tell me?" his mom warned.

"I promise," Nick said. "I've read up on all the pitchers who weren't careful after serious arm injuries and never recovered."

She hugged him to her and planted a kiss on his cheek. "You really did scare me," she said, almost like a reprimand.

"I'll try not to do it again."

"Get out of the way next time!"

"Oh, sure," Nick said, slapping a palm to his forehead. *"Now you tell me."*

He planned to meet Ben and Diego at the field after lunch the next day. Ben had already made Nick swear on their friendship that he wasn't trying to hide an injury.

"I swear," Nick said on the phone. "Honestly, I'm fine."

But knowing Ben, he'd have to prove it to him on the field.

In baseball, you always did.

Nick raced out of his apartment the next morning, ready to get out into the summer air after being cooped up for twenty-four hours. Before he left the building, he knocked on Mrs. G's door.

"Everything all right?" she asked.

"Yes," Nick said. "I just wanted to thank you for what you did for me. You're like my guardian angel."

"And I always will be," she said, winking.

"I gotta tell you, Mrs. G. After that hit, I thought my season was shot."

"I keep telling you, Nicolás," she said. "That's not the way your story is supposed to end."

On the way to Macombs Dam Park, he carried an old baseball, feeling the seams, rolling it around in his hand, adhering the grip that he used for his fastball.

"He's baaaaaaack," Diego said when he saw Nick coming up the sidewalk.

"Back from where?" Nick yelled. "I didn't go anyplace."

When he arrived at the field, he set his equipment down near the bench on the third-base side of the field.

"How we lookin'?" Ben said.

"Fine," Nick said. "Same as we were lookin' when you asked last night and then again this morning."

"If you'd really gotten hurt and missed the rest of the tournament," Diego said, "that pretty much would have ruined my whole summer."

"*His* summer," Nick said to Ben, jerking a thumb at Diego.

"All about him," Ben said.

Diego grinned. "Why do you think I wear number one?" he said. "It's like my uncle, the one who plays the trumpet, always says: if you don't blow your own horn, then there is no music."

They formed a triangle in the infield and did some light throwing. Nick felt no pull behind his shoulder, no pain, no nothing. Just sweet relief. He'd promised Ben that he wouldn't do any real throwing today. But he made a deal with himself that if he remained pain-free, and didn't require a return trip to see Mrs. G, he would have a throw day tomorrow.

They all kept track of the standings on the Dream League website. So far, the Blazers were the only undefeated team. The Giants, Eric Dobbs's team, were right behind them, with their one loss having been to the Blazers. But if both teams won out the rest of the way, it would be Nick against Eric with a championship on the line, and maybe a trip across the street.

Fine with me, Nick thought.

Ben kept repeating the same line: "You beat him once. We beat him once. You can do it again and so can we."

Nick wanted to try out hitting, to see if swinging a bat affected his shoulder at all. Turned out it didn't. On the Blazers, they frequently talked about what a great closer Kenny Locke was, and how many saves he'd gotten in the tournament. But maybe the biggest save in Nick's season belonged to Mrs. G.

Nick planned to invite her to the championship game if the Blazers made it. And if he got to throw that first pitch at Yankee Stadium, Nick wanted her to see that, too. So she could witness firsthand how his baseball story ended, at least for the time being.

After Nick, Ben, and Diego practiced fielding grounders and fly balls, and even some bunting drills, Diego announced that he wanted Ben to pitch while he tried to hit left-handed.

"Please don't do this," Ben said.

"You know how bad you look when you try to be a switch-hitter," Nick reminded him.

"Today is going to be different," Diego said. "I can feel it."

"My mom taught me the definition of insanity," Ben said. "It's doing the same thing over and over again but expecting a different result each time."

"Just a few swings," Diego said. "Promise."

The swings did not go well. The best Diego could do was a slow roller back to the pitcher's mound before he finally gave up.

Ben looked at Nick. "Think you'll ever be able to unsee that swing?" he said.

"Never."

Ben nodded. "Same."

"It looked like he was trying to swat away a swarm of bees," Nick said.

"Or like someone swinging at a piñata blindfolded," Ben said.

"You guys finished?" Diego said, leaning on his bat.

Ben laughed. "Why, you want some more?"

"You guys treat me like I'm the piñata!" Diego said.

They sat there in the grass, their backs to the high fence behind home plate, sipping from their water bottles, looking out at the empty field before them and all the familiar sights: the nearby fields, the subway tracks above River Avenue, the huge New Balance billboard. Nick would remember so many things about this neighborhood when he was living somewhere else someday. But this part of the world, the view from this field, was what he would remember the very best. Some of his happiest memories were made here.

"Why can't it just be like this?" Nick said.

"Like what?" Ben said.

"Like . . . I don't know. Normal."

"This *is* normal," Diego said.

"I mean all the time," Nick said, falling back into the grass, placing a hand under his head. "You guys talk about me like I'm this brilliant baseball player, even though you're both as good as I am. But it's like you'd rather be me, or something."

He wasn't saying it to be boastful, and Ben and Diego knew it. They both sat quiet while Nick vented.

He had his glove in his lap, turning it over in his hands, noticing a new place that might require some sewing before the Blazers' next game.

"But the truth is," he continued, "I want to be you guys."

"Then you wouldn't be *you*," Diego said. "You wouldn't be a pitcher."

"He's not just talking about baseball," Ben said.

"Look, I'm not saying that everything is perfect in your lives," Nick said. "I'm not an idiot. I know everybody has stuff they'd like to change." He paused. "But look at you, Ben. Your grandparents came over from Ireland. I know you say you're Irish American. But people don't look at you that way. They just see you as being *American* American."

"So are you," Ben said. "We're both American."

"It's different," Nick said.

"I know," said Ben, respecting Nick's point of view. "But not everyone who came here back then had it so great. Most probably didn't. From what my parents have told me, people looked at my grandparents as a bunch of lousy job stealers. They'd show up looking for jobs and see signs that said, 'No Irish Need Apply.'"

"I get that," Nick said. "But nobody was looking to arrest them once they got here. And, Diego, because you're second-generation American, you don't have to worry, because your parents are American citizens."

"Same as your mom and dad will be someday," Diego assured him. "The way you and Amelia already are."

"But we're just as likely to be sent back to the DR," Nick said. "Well, my parents would be sent back. I'd be going for the first time."

"Maybe if it hasn't happened yet, it never will," Ben said, trying to sound positive.

"Or it could happen tomorrow," said Nick.

In the distance, they saw that two kids about their age had shown up to play catch on the field closest to River Avenue.

"I just feel so powerless," Nick said.

"I hear you," Ben said.

"But no matter what happens," Diego said, "you've got us."

"And Marisol, too," Ben said. "Don't forget that."

"Yeah, but she doesn't know about my family, and I can't bring myself to tell her," Nick said. "Her dad's a New York City cop. If Marisol ever let slip anything about my dad, what's to stop Officer Pérez from showing up at our door and arresting him?"

In the very next moment, from behind them, a voice said, "You really think I would do that?"

Nick didn't have to turn around to know who the voice belonged to.

When he finally did turn to face her, Nick saw the hurt in Marisol's eyes. She stood behind the fence, and Nick saw her shove something quickly into her back pocket.

"You trust me that little?" she said, on the verge of tears. "Or maybe you don't trust me at all."

Nick stood up.

"That's not what I meant," he said.

"That's what it sounded like to me."

"Let me explain," Nick said, looking for the nearest opening in the fence so he could get to her before she walked away.

"You've already said more than enough," she said, taking a step back.

Then, as Nick ran toward the gate to his left, Marisol ran the other way, toward Yankee Stadium.

28

Nick knew she was fast, having watched her on the tennis courts. He just didn't know *how* fast.

Marisol ran at full speed, not once looking back even as Nick shouted at her to stop. But she finally had to when she missed the light at 161st Street, which Nick knew from experience was a long one. It was a wide, busy street where traffic seemed to be coming from all directions.

"Marisol," Nick said when he caught up to her. "At least hear me out."

"I don't want to hear anything you have to say to me," she said, turning her back to him.

"I didn't know you were listening," Nick reasoned.

"Obviously."

Now the light changed.

"Please don't make me chase you," he said. "I might pull a muscle."

He grinned at her sheepishly.

"Go try to be funny with your friends," she said.

That burned. "You're my friend."

"Not anymore," she spat.

Another punch in the gut. The second big blow of the week.

"You don't mean that," he said.

"I told you how I felt about you keeping secrets from me," she said.

"But what you heard—that's a secret from just about everybody outside my family," Nick said, desperate for her to understand.

"Not Ben and Diego," she said, arms crossed.

"But they're like family to me," Nick said. As soon as it was out of his mouth, he knew it was the wrong response.

"And I'm not," Marisol said. It wasn't a question.

She was right. She didn't feel like family to him. But how could he explain that to her without making a fool of himself all over again? Ben and Diego *were* like brothers. But he would never think of Marisol as a sister. His feelings for her, even though he didn't always understand them, were different. A lot.

Nick wrapped a hand around his neck. "My dad wasn't happy when I told Ben and Diego," he said. "But that was before immigration policies starting changing. It's not safe anymore, and now I'm not allowed to tell anybody else. Not even you."

He hoped she would understand the circumstances. Understand why he couldn't tell her. "Please don't go," he said, reaching for her hand.

She didn't take it, but agreed to listen to his side. They walked over to some steps leading out of the parking garage behind them. Nick sat down and Marisol, almost reluctantly, dropped down beside him.

At least she was still here. For now that felt like a lot.

"It's nothing against you," Nick said. "My dad says the more people who know, the more dangerous it could become for us."

"So this is all on your dad?" she said.

"You don't do what your dad tells you to?" Nick said.

"He's a police officer," she said.

"And what, my dad's a criminal?"

The words were out of his mouth before he could force them back in.

"That's not fair," Marisol said, clearly insulted.

"You're right," Nick said. "I'm sorry."

"And I'm sorry you didn't think you could trust me," she said, "no matter what your dad says."

"It's not like that," Nick said. "I'm just so terrified of the police and what they could do."

"But you're not your parents and I'm not mine," Marisol said. She seemed to have calmed down a bit. "You know me. And if you know me, you have to know that I would never tell your secret to anyone, certainly not my dad."

Nick might have stopped running a few minutes ago, but his heart thudded in his chest as if he'd just completed a marathon.

"Listen. I wasn't keeping secrets from you to hurt you. You have to know that," he said.

"I just can't believe you thought I'd go running to my dad."

Nick simply said, "You don't know what it's like to be afraid all the time."

"You're right," she said. "I don't."

"It's not that I thought you'd try to get my family in trouble," he said. "I'm just not sure how any of this works. If your dad would have to report my dad or something."

Neither of them said anything for a beat. Then Nick said, "Can I ask you something?"

She shrugged, as if not caring whether he did or didn't.

"Why were you even at the field today?"

"Because I wanted to surprise you," she said, "with *these*."

She reached into her back pocket and came out with a pair of tickets.

Yankee tickets.

"These are for Michael Arroyo's next start," she said. "Against the Red Sox next week. My dad wanted us to go to the game together."

Nick looked at the tickets in her hand, then back to her, speechless.

"Section one fourteen," she said. "Behind the Yankee dugout."

Nick felt like one of those cartoon characters with their eyes bugging out of their head.

"How did your dad get such good tickets?" Nick asked.

"That was supposed to be part of the surprise," she said. "He got them from Michael Arroyo."

If Nick was stunned by the tickets, he was absolutely floored by this piece of news.

"Wait . . ." Nick said, taking a second to wrap his head around what he'd just heard. "Your dad *knows* Michael?"

"From when he does overtime work at Yankee Stadium," she said.

"You never told me that."

"I guess that was my secret." She wasn't smiling or laughing, and Nick knew their relationship had suffered a big, terrible blow. He just hoped that, like his shoulder, it could be repaired. It wouldn't be painless, but he couldn't afford to lose her.

She handed Nick the tickets, got up off the steps, and walked away. This time, she caught the light on 161st Street and crossed without looking back. Almost as if she didn't notice Yankee Stadium right there in front of her. As if it wasn't there at all.

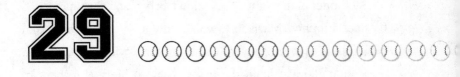

NICK TRIED CALLING MARISOL WHEN HE GOT HOME, TO SAY THAT IF she didn't want to go to the game with him, he'd return the tickets so she could take someone else.

It was the right thing to do.

But his call went straight to voice mail, and he wasn't about to leave a long message that she might not listen to anyway, so all he said was, "It's me. Please call."

Later, he went over their argument in his head, and came to the conclusion that it wasn't all his fault. Marisol had no right to sneak up on him and basically eavesdrop on a private conversation he was having with Ben and Diego. But even Nick knew how lame that sounded. Regardless of how it happened, he'd said what he said and Marisol had heard him. Now Nick had to accept it, and figure out a way to make things right. If he ever got the chance. But she would have to accept his side, too. After all, he had his reasons—good ones—for not telling Marisol about his family. She'd have to understand Nick's decision if they were going to continue being friends.

Nick briefly considered writing her an email. He was better in writing, more thoughtful. And he'd be able to choose his words more carefully.

More than anything, Nick wanted Marisol to know that he'd never meant to hurt her.

At dinner that night, Nick didn't bring up what happened between him and Marisol. It would only upset his parents, and Nick couldn't stomach anyone else being angry with him right now.

If he could just hand the tickets back to Marisol in person, at least he'd have an excuse to see her again. Even if it meant he wouldn't get to see Michael Arroyo pitch against the Red Sox.

"How was your day?" Nick's dad asked at one point.

"Same old, same old," Nick said. "Ben and Diego and I played some ball at the field."

"When I was your age," Victor García said, "my parents would pack me a lunch and I would go off in the morning to play baseball and not come back home until dinnertime." He smiled. "We didn't know how good we had it."

Amelia, Nick noticed, wasn't eating very much tonight. She was pushing food around on her plate, but rarely putting any in her mouth. He thought she looked unusually tired. Even the simple act of eating dinner was exhausting her. This wasn't totally out of the ordinary, but it concerned Nick nonetheless.

"You okay, sis?" Nick asked.

"Just felt a little drained all day," she said. "Was gonna go out for a walk, but my legs were sore."

This was more information than she usually gave out, to Nick or their parents. She pushed her chair back, said she wasn't hungry, and excused herself.

"Don't worry about me. I'll feel better in the morning," she said before dragging herself over to the couch and clicking on the TV.

When Nick finished clearing the dishes, he went to his room, sat down at his desk, and opened his laptop to a new document. He started writing a letter to Marisol, wondering if he'd ever build up the courage to send it.

He was midway through the letter when his dad suddenly burst into the room.

"Amelia needs to see a doctor," he said before turning on his heel.

"When?"

"*Now!*" Victor García said.

A lot of things happened all at once. Amelia's breathing was erratic, her legs swelled up, and she had a 102-degree fever.

"We're going to the Montefiore Urgent Care," Victor García said. "I'll take her."

They had been there before. Nick knew it was a haul, even if you took a car service.

"I'll go with you," Nick's mom said.

"You've done this so many times when I was working," Nick's dad said. "I'm here tonight. I'll take her."

"I'll go with you," Nick said.

"You don't have to," Amelia said weakly.

"I want to," Nick said.

The Einstein Free Clinic was only open a couple of days a week, and occasionally at night. But Montefiore Urgent Care, up past Fordham Heights near the Bronx Zoo, was open twenty-four hours, seven days a week.

Nick ran down to Mrs. G's apartment, told her that Amelia was sick and that they needed a ride to urgent care. Mrs. G immediately called her nephew, but he said he was on a driving job up on

White Plains Road and wouldn't be back for at least another hour.

Mrs. G told Nick she would order an Uber instead.

"*You* have an Uber account?" Nick said, aghast.

"I am more modern than you think, my young friend."

When the car arrived at their building, Nick jumped into the front seat, and his dad and Amelia slid into the back. Fortunately, traffic was light this time of night on the Grand Concourse, and the ride only took them about twenty minutes.

Amelia's legs buckled when she got out of the car in front of the big URGENT CARE sign.

Victor García picked up his daughter as easily as he would a stack of folded clothes and carried her toward the door.

From the corner of his eye, Nick caught sight of a big, heavy-set guy lumbering toward the door. His shirt was torn in a couple of spots, and he appeared, to Nick, pretty wobbly, tripping over his own feet and muttering under his breath. Nick picked up his pace to get ahead of the man, opening the door wide for his dad and Amelia to pass through.

"Hey," the man said, his words slurred. "I was here first."

Nick saw there was blood on the front of his shirt, and a gash over his left eye. He looked like someone who'd just lost a fight.

"No, sir," Nick said, holding the door open for him to be polite. "We were here first. My sister is sick."

"Think I care?" the man said behind him.

For some reason, the man laughed as Victor García carried Amelia through the door. Once they were all inside, the man again tried to rush ahead of Nick's dad. But he wasn't moving very well, stumbling across the lobby.

"Hey!" the man yelled to the woman behind the welcome desk. "These people are trying to cut the line here."

Nick's dad, still holding Amelia, turned and gave a piercing glare.

"We were here first," Victor García said, keeping himself and his voice calm.

"You people," the man said, shaking his head. Then he started grumbling to himself, and staggered over to one of the chairs in the waiting area. He fell into it so hard, Nick was surprised the chair didn't break.

Victor García asked Amelia if she thought she could stand on her own. She nodded, and he set her down gently. Nick stood beside her, looping an elbow through hers just in case she needed support. Then his dad leaned forward and spoke through a small window to the nurse behind the desk, making sure he could pay cash for the visit. Nick's dad had brought the "emergency money" he kept in a box on the shelf of his bedroom closet.

After filling out some paperwork, Nick's dad and Amelia disappeared through some double doors, leaving Nick in the waiting room. The large man who'd followed them in was at the window now, talking to the nurse, and then a few minutes later he, too, was escorted back to see a doctor.

Nick sat patiently in the waiting area. Every so often, another person would walk through the front door. Sometimes with a sick child in need of medical attention. Other times admitting themselves. His dad and Amelia were gone so long, that the man with the cut over his eye was out before they were, his head now bandaged in white gauze and tape. Nick hadn't been around many drunk people in his life, but he was pretty sure that's what the man was.

He was just glad to see the man walk out the front door and out of their lives.

Victor and Amelia finally came back through the double doors. Amelia's breathing had returned to normal. She still had a slight fever, but her temperature had gone down, and the doctor had given them a prescription for a "nonsteroid anti-inflammatory" medicine that would reduce the swelling in her legs.

"*Non*steroid," Amelia said to Nick. "It means I can still play for the Yankees if I want to."

"Good one, sis," Nick said.

Nick and his dad walked on either side of Amelia as they made their way outside the urgent care center. Nick's dad didn't want to trouble Mrs. G for another Uber ride, and said he'd rather not wait for one anyway. A taxi was faster, and he had more than enough cash left to get home.

They were standing on the sidewalk near the street, Victor with his arm out to flag down a cab, when the big man came stumbling back toward them.

"What makes you people think you're better than me?" the man said.

You people, Nick thought.

He knew what the man meant.

People who didn't look like him.

"That girl looks fine to me," the man said, gesturing to Amelia. "I was the one with the head wound."

"Please stop bothering us," Victor García said. "We mean you no harm. I'm just trying to get my daughter home."

Nick's eyes were on his father's now, and he saw something in them he didn't often see: anger.

"Maybe," the man said, "you're the one bothering *me*, Pedro."

Nick saw his father's fists clench. "My name is Victor," his dad said.

Standing so close to him, Nick could see the man was much larger than his father. Not so much in height, but certainly in weight. The man's face was beet-red, and he bobbed slightly from side to side. He took one fumbling step closer to Victor García and, as he did, knocked Amelia aside, like he didn't notice her standing there. Amelia lost her balance and almost went down, but Nick caught her by the hip.

"Hey!" Nick said.

"Not talking to you, boy," the man said.

Victor García whispered to Nick, "You and Amelia, step away."

He turned to the man and said, "No seas tonto."

"What do you mean, tonto?" the man said. "Like the one in the *Lone Ranger* movie?"

"It means 'fool,'" Victor García said.

At that, the man swung at Nick's father.

It was a wild swing, one the man had telegraphed, and Nick's dad easily avoided it. But missing the punch just seemed to make the big man angrier. He clumsily lowered his shoulder and drove into Victor, bringing them both violently to the ground.

With Victor García pinned beneath him, the man grunted,

throwing punch after punch, which Nick's dad somehow managed to block with his hands and forearms. Nick's dad always said that fighting proved nothing, and solved nothing. He refused to fight the man back.

"Stop it!" Amelia yelled now.

Nick's head whipped around, looking for anybody who could step in and break this up. His instinct was to run back into the urgent care center, but he couldn't leave Amelia or his dad.

To Nick's relief, a security guard came running out of the facility. At the same time, police sirens could be heard in the distance, closely followed by flashing lights on the Grand Concourse.

A police car pulled up to the curb, the doors opening before the car had come to a complete stop. Two officers clad in navy-blue uniforms came out—one a tall, lanky guy uttering something into his walkie, the other an older, beefy man carrying two sets of handcuffs. Together, they pulled the big man to his feet and cuffed his wrists behind his back. Then they lifted Victor García up, and Nick could see the younger cop readying the other set of handcuffs.

"Dad," Nick said.

Victor quickly reached into his pocket and handed Nick two twenty-dollar bills. "Get your sister home," he said, before the bulkier officer pushed his arms behind him, clicking the handcuffs into place.

Nick and Amelia watched in utter astonishment. Both men arrested, even though Victor García hadn't thrown a single punch.

30

"I SHOULD CALL MOM," NICK SAID AS THE OFFICERS LED VICTOR TO a second patrol car that had now arrived on the scene. The other man had already been loaded into the first.

"Call her from the cab," his dad called over his shoulder. "Just go."

Nick craned his neck and spotted a few vacant yellow cabs up the street, but none of them were stopping. Probably because the drivers didn't want to be anywhere near police cars. The first set of policemen used the delay to ask Nick and Amelia about the fight, while a third took notes.

"Why did you arrest my dad?" Nick asked in a panic. "He didn't do anything wrong."

"Son," the older policeman said, "your dad and the other man got into a fight in front of a hospital."

"It wasn't a fight, though!" Nick said, trying to keep his voice even. "The only one throwing punches was the other guy. My dad was just trying to protect himself. And us."

"I'm sure it will all get sorted out once they get processed at the precinct," the officer said.

"Will he have to spend the night in jail?" Amelia asked, and until he heard her speak, Nick had almost forgotten she was there. After everything Amelia had been through tonight, Nick couldn't believe she was still standing.

"He might," the taller officer said.

Nick knew his next question sounded stupid, but he had to ask. "Our dad has definitely been arrested, though, right?"

"You just saw it happen," the policeman said.

I saw it happen, Nick thought. He couldn't deny it because he saw it with his own two eyes. His worst nightmare come to life.

Finally, the cops helped Nick and Amelia hail a cab. Once inside, Nick called their mom from his cell, the words pouring out of him in a rush.

"Dios mío," she said.

Then she asked about Amelia and Nick handed his sister the phone.

"Mom," she said, "I'm fine."

None of them were.

They were shocked when, a few hours later, Victor García came walking into the apartment. Nick's mom ran to the door before it was open all the way and threw her arms around her husband, gripping him tightly around the neck.

"Gracias a Dios," she said.

"Don't thank Him yet," Victor García said, throwing an arm over Nick and Amelia.

He looked sad, tired, and angry all at once.

"What happened when you got to the precinct?" Amelia asked.

"Felt like I was right back where I was nearly twenty years ago," their dad said. "They gave me a DAT and released me."

"DAT?" Nick asked.

"Desk appearance ticket," Victor García said. "It means I'll be arraigned at the big courthouse down the block in a couple of weeks. If ICE doesn't come for me first."

"It's not fair!" Nick cried. "The other man is the one who started everything."

He knew he sounded silly, like a petulant child who didn't get his way. But he couldn't contain himself. Rage boiled up inside him.

"The other man claimed I was the one who instigated the fight," Victor García said. "I tried to defend my side, but the cops didn't want to hear it. They told me I'd get my chance to tell it to the judge."

They sat down as a family once again at the kitchen table, where they'd been just hours earlier, before Amelia had fallen ill.

His dad sighed. "They took my fingerprints."

"But that's normal, right?" Nick said.

"It is, but that's not the problem," his dad said. "The problem is that now my fingerprints are all over the system. Now anyone will be able to see that I was arrested before."

"'Anyone' meaning ICE," Amelia said, in a voice so soft Nick could barely hear it.

"Yes," their dad said, sounding more defeated than Nick had ever heard him.

Nick didn't hesitate. He got up from the table, ran to his room, opened the bottom drawer, and came back with Mr. Gasson's card. He slapped it on the table in front of his dad, then turned it over and pointed to where Mr. Gasson had written his cell phone number.

"You need to call him, Dad," Nick said.

"Nick's right," Amelia said. "You need a lawyer. Someone who's dealt with this before."

Their dad picked up the card. He looked up at the ceiling, then exhaled a long breath. "All right," he said.

"Mr. Gasson said you could call at any time of the day or night," Nick said.

"It is past midnight now," Victor García said. "I promise to call him first thing in the morning."

It turned out first thing wasn't early enough.

ICE came for Victor García at eight o'clock the following morning. Graciela García had already gone off to work. Nick and Amelia stood helplessly by, watching their father being taken away by the men in the blue vests. They plowed into the apartment like they owned the place. Five armed officials in heavy boots, stomping across the floor to the kitchen, where Victor García sat drinking his café con leche. Nick ran into his bedroom to find the flyer Mr. Gasson had given him, the one about their rights. But Victor García had no rights now. Not after the second set of handcuffs in two days was slapped onto his wrists. Two ICE agents ushered him out the door before Nick or Amelia could even say goodbye.

"Where are you taking our dad?" Nick asked one of the officials lagging behind.

"Bergen County Jail," one of the ICE men said. "In Hackensack, New Jersey."

Then the crew was out the door. Amelia and Nick rushed over to the window, where they could see their father being led down the steps to a van parked in front of the building.

Nick raced into the kitchen then, picking up the card his dad never got to use, and dialed Ryan Gasson's number.

31

MR. GASSON PICKED UP ON THE FIRST RING. HE SAID HE WAS IN court until the afternoon, but would stop by their apartment later that evening. By then Graciela García would be home from work. She'd wanted to come back as soon as Nick gave her the news, but he assured her that he and Amelia were fine, and there was nothing for any of them to do until Mr. Gasson showed up.

Around five o'clock, Ryan Gasson buzzed downstairs, and Nick and Amelia greeted him at the door. Their mom offered him a drink, and he accepted a mug of hot coffee. The four of them sat together on the large L-shaped couch while Nick and Amelia recounted how everything went down, from the time they'd arrived at the urgent care center until the ICE agents barged into their apartment that morning.

"Our dad is innocent," Nick said to Mr. Gasson. "The other man started the fight; he nearly knocked down Amelia!"

"There's no doubt in my mind that your dad is innocent," Mr. Gasson said. "But the government doesn't care about that now, or what really happened last night. In their eyes, his guilt began when he and your mom stayed in this country after their tourist visas expired."

"I just want to see my husband," their mom said to Mr. Gasson, her voice faltering.

"I'm afraid that's not a very good idea, Mrs. García," Mr. Gasson said. "It would be too risky for you to show up in New Jersey. You'd be questioned about your own citizenship. It's actually lucky you weren't in the apartment when they showed up this morning."

"You mean they could have arrested me, too?" Graciela said, a little shocked.

"Yes, ma'am, they could've."

"Then what would happen to my children?"

"Exactly," Mr. Gasson said. Nick thought about Michael Arroyo then. How he and his brother evaded child protective services when their dad's passing left them orphaned in New York. He might have wound up in the same situation with Amelia.

"You have to find a way to help our dad," Nick said.

"It's what I do," Mr. Gasson said. "By law I can't see him until he's been in New Jersey for at least twenty-four hours. Sometimes forty-eight hours. But the minute I can see him, I'll be there, I promise."

He stood up then, and shook Graciela's hand.

"If I don't call later, I'll call tomorrow," he said.

"Where are you going now?" Nick asked.

"To get your dad on the phone and tell him the cavalry's on its way."

"Cavalry?" Nick said.

"Like I told you," Mr. Gasson said. "The good guys."

32

A FEW NIGHTS LATER NICK CAME INTO THE LIVING ROOM TO TELL his mom and Amelia he was quitting the Blazers.

"No," they said at once.

"I can't be thinking about baseball when we're worrying every minute about Dad," he said. "It's selfish."

"You are not quitting your team," his mom said. "Your father would never hear of it."

"Playing baseball seems silly right now," Nick said. "And it doesn't do anything to help Dad."

"I don't want to hear another word about it," his mother said. "You're not quitting, and you best hope I don't tell your father you were considering it."

Once a day, Victor García was granted a phone call to his wife. They were limited to only a few minutes, as there were others at the detention center waiting to use the phone. But at least Nick's parents were able to communicate.

"He doesn't want us to put our lives on pause," Nick's mom said. "And, Nicolás? That means playing in this tournament."

"It still feels wrong to me," Nick said, shaking his head.

"It's senseless to give up something you love in the name of *somebody* you love," she said. "And believe me, it would disappoint your father more than anything."

The three of them sat in the living room quietly, the absence of Victor García felt by all. Nick muted the Yankee game on TV.

It was Amelia who finally spoke.

"I remember something Michael Arroyo said in that documentary you made me watch," Amelia said. "He said that when he and his brother were afraid of being separated and put into foster care, baseball was his safe place, same as you always tell me it's yours."

"I didn't even know you were paying attention," Nick said, surprised, and honestly a little impressed.

"And," his sister continued, "when they took baseball away from him after he couldn't produce his birth certificate, he described how terrible it was to lose that safe place."

The Blazers' next game was scheduled for the following night, against the Astros. Nick wasn't pitching, just playing second base.

"Your hero would never have given up baseball," Amelia said. "And neither will you."

Nick felt a smile come over him, and he started to laugh.

"What?" Amelia said.

"I was just thinking of something Ben said to Diego once," he said.

"What was that?"

"I hate it when you're right."

33

NICK'S MOM GOT A CALL FROM MR. GASSON AN HOUR BEFORE IT was time for Nick to leave for the Blazers-Astros game.

She put him on speaker so Nick and Amelia could hear.

"How is my husband?" Graciela asked.

"Even tougher than you said he was," Mr. Gasson said.

Graciela smiled. "Do you have any good news for us?"

Mr. Gasson shook his head. "I'm sorry to say I don't."

Nick piped up. "What happens next?"

"For now," he said, "your dad has to stay put. It can be two to three months before he gets a court appearance in front of an immigration judge. Possibly longer. For now, all he's done is meet with a deportation agent."

Graciela García lifted a hand to her mouth when she heard the word "deportation."

"Everybody is just following the laws as written," Mr. Gasson said, trying to reassure her.

"They're treating our dad like a criminal," Amelia said, "even though he's the farthest thing from."

"I'm pretty sure that's clear to everyone who's met him over there," Mr. Gasson said. "Unfortunately, all that matters is what the judge thinks. The rest is simply following protocol."

"So what do we do now?" Nick asked.

"I've got some ideas," Mr. Gasson said, his voice sounding tinny over speakerphone. "But for now, I don't want to give you false hope."

"My dad says that's the worst kind," Nick said.

Mr. Gasson chuckled. "He actually told me the same thing when I was with him today."

"Did he say anything else?" Nick's mom asked.

"Yeah," Mr. Gasson said. "He told Nick to win his game tonight."

Baseball felt different tonight, and not just because Nick wasn't pitching.

Always Nick had loved the walk to Macombs Dam Park, down from the Grand Concourse to 161st, the Bronx County Courthouse towering above, looking like the Yankee Stadium of courthouses. Often he'd clutch a ball in his hand, getting himself ready, feeling as if he were carrying the whole night in his hand.

Tonight he didn't bring a ball. He wasn't pitching, but it was more than that. His dad was sitting in a New Jersey detention center, which Nick knew was just another term for jail. The tournament, MVP award, pitching at Yankee Stadium—these all felt like childish dreams compared to what he now desired more than anything: getting his father back.

Coach Viera didn't comment on Nick's dad when Nick arrived at the field. Likely, he knew and just didn't feel comfortable mentioning it. Or it was possible he hadn't heard. Either way, Nick wasn't going to bring it up. Word usually spread pretty quickly around their Bronx neighborhood. If someone had a baby or got married, Nick's parents would hear about it within a few days, through a friend, or a neighbor, or a colleague. Like one massive game of telephone. What happened to Victor García was a big deal, and Nick wasn't naive. Most of the community would have heard about it by now, and that included Nick's teammates. At this point, after Nick had worked so hard to keep the secret, it was almost a relief to have it out in the open—if also a tremendous burden.

Because while he appreciated everyone's sympathy, that didn't mean he wanted to discuss the matter more than he already had—the exceptions being Ben and Diego.

"We'll get through this together," Ben said after the two of them finished stretching for batting practice.

"Like we always do," Diego said, sidling up next to them. "Your mom and Amelia coming tonight?"

"Mom is, but Amelia wasn't feeling great, so she's staying home."

After all she'd endured, both physically and emotionally, Nick couldn't blame his sister. Yet between the two of them, Amelia remained the most realistic about their situation. No matter how much she talked about prayer and belief and happy endings, she'd done enough research on immigration and the policies of the current administration to know how most of these stories ended.

"You sure you're okay to play?" Ben asked.

"My mom and Amelia were right," Nick said. "I *have* to play."

He looked over now and saw his mom taking her seat in the third row of the bleachers. Even from where he sat on the Blazers' bench, Nick could see it took all her strength to come out here.

But if she can stay strong and my dad can stay strong, Nick kept telling himself, *so can I.*

From the top of the first inning, Nick treated this game as if it were the biggest he'd ever play in his life. He led the infield chatter behind Kelvin, the Blazers' starting pitcher tonight, as he got the Astros in order. Coach had Nick leading off, so when Kelvin struck out the Astros' number three hitter, Nick sprinted back to the Blazers' bench. Then he hit the first pitch he got from Mel Mora, the Astros' starting pitcher, into right-center field. Nick made a big turn at first, and when he noticed the right fielder was a little slow getting to the ball, he turned on the jets to stretch what should have been a single into a double.

When Diego flied out to right field, Nick tagged and made it to third easily. Ben singled him home, and then Darryl hit a home run to give the Blazers a 3–0 lead.

"Dude," Diego said on the bench. "You are on *fire* tonight."

"If I'm gonna take stuff out on somebody," Nick said, "it might as well be the other team."

Nick ended up with four hits by the end of the night, the Blazers winning 11–3. After the handshake line, Coach pulled him aside.

"Are you okay?" he said.

"Coach," Nick said, "we won big, and I was four-for-four."

"I've just never seen you this fired up before," Coach said. "I know how much you want to win, but you rarely show it on the outside."

"Sometimes," Nick said, "you gotta cut loose and let everybody know how much you love the game."

Then Coach announced he was taking the team for ice cream again, and the parents were invited to come along. Nick's mom said she wanted to get home to Amelia. So Nick and the rest of the Blazers led the way to the new ice cream shop next to Stan's Sports World on River Avenue, while a handful of parents tagged behind.

At the end of the night, Nick and Ben dropped Diego at his building, and then Nick dropped Ben off at his.

As Nick turned for home, Ben put a hand on his shoulder. "Wait," he said. "There's something I want to tell you."

"Make it something good," Nick said. "Can't handle any more bad news right now."

Ben stood there, trying to find the right words. Finally, he lifted his shoulders and let them drop, blew out some air, and said, "If anything happens to your dad, my mom says you can live with us."

Nick started to say something, but Ben held up a hand.

"Amelia, too," he said.

"You told your mom?" Nick said, a little embarrassed.

"Didn't have to," Ben said.

Of course, Nick thought. Everyone knew by now.

"I don't know what to say," Nick said. "Except that's about the nicest thing anybody's ever said to me."

Ben shrugged like it was no big thing. "You'd do the same for me."

"Still," Nick said.

Ben told him to call or text, no matter how late, with any news about his dad. Good or bad.

Nick walked up the Grand Concourse, deciding he wasn't ready to go upstairs yet, and crossed the street into Joyce Kilmer Park. He found an empty bench and plunked himself down. In front of him, two boys who looked no more than five or six were chasing a soccer ball, giggling and out of breath, while their mother looked on, snapping pictures. Nick envied them: carefree and innocent.

He watched them and occasionally checked his phone for any messages from his mom or Amelia or Mr. Gasson. But there were none.

Nick didn't know how long he sat on that bench, but it was getting dark fast, so he got up and made his way toward the park exit. He was cautious to look both ways before crossing the busy two-way street on a light. Just one of the many things he was taught to be careful of.

Not that being careful had done any good.

He didn't see Marisol standing in front of his building until he nearly knocked into her.

He made no attempt to hide his pleasure at seeing her, though.

"I know you," he said. "You're the tennis girl."

Marisol cut to the chase. "I know," she said.

"About my dad, you mean," Nick said.

"Yes," she said, her lips pinched. "Nick, I'm so sorry."

The words were simple, yet they said so much. Sorry about his dad, sorry about the way they'd left things hanging, sorry about the misunderstandings.

"Me too," Nick said.

Then Marisol threw her arms around his neck and leaned her

head against his shoulder. Nick was overwhelmed. He'd never hugged a girl other than his sister. And he'd never been this close to Marisol, but it felt right. He locked his arms around her waist and they held each other for a good few seconds.

When they broke apart, she said, "If you still have those tickets, I'd very much like to go with you to the Michael Arroyo game."

34 ⦿⦿⦿⦿⦿⦿⦿⦿⦿⦿⦿⦿⦿

MR. GASSON CALLED THE HOME PHONE THE NEXT MORNING WHEN Nick was getting ready to meet Ben and Diego at the field. Graciela was working and Amelia was over at a friend's, so it was just Nick alone in the apartment.

Nick asked Mr. Gasson if he could accompany him to New Jersey the next time he went to visit his dad.

"Your dad doesn't want you to see him there," Mr. Gasson said. "He's been pretty firm about that."

"I just want to be there for him."

"You are," Mr. Gasson said, "even if you're not there physically."

"Are you making any progress?" Nick asked.

"I've got a plan, put it that way," Mr. Gasson said. "Doing everything I can."

"Thank you."

"Don't thank me yet," Mr. Gasson said. "I haven't done anything. If this were a baseball game, we'd only be in the early innings."

Then Nick changed the subject and told Mr. Gasson he was going to Yankee Stadium to watch Michael Arroyo pitch against the Red Sox.

"Wow," Mr. Gasson said. "I'm jealous. Good seats?"

"Really good."

"Who are you going with?"

Nick felt a smile come over him.

"A friend," he said.

Marisol's parents and Nick's mom arranged for Nick and Marisol to walk to the Stadium alone on Tuesday night. The first pitch, as always, was scheduled for a little before seven o'clock. After the game, Officer Pérez, who was working at the Stadium, would walk them home.

On the way to the game, Marisol said to Nick, "I want to apologize again for the way I acted."

She was wearing the new Yankees cap her dad had bought her, her dark-brown hair tied in two long braids.

"I was wrong," she said. "I understand now why you had to keep your dad's secret."

"In the end, it didn't help him," Nick said. "ICE still came, and now he's stuck in jail for the next few months, at least."

"It's not right," Marisol said, shaking her head.

"Which part?"

"Every part," she said. "But I've had a lot of time to think about what happened between us. I know you were just trying to protect your family. That's why I'm sorry if I hurt your feelings."

"But I hurt yours first by not trusting you with my secret," Nick said.

"It wasn't only your secret to tell," she replied. "I should have respected that."

"But—"

"Let's just agree to keep it real, okay?" Marisol said.

Nick nodded. "Deal," he said, and smiled. "Real deal."

"Good, so it's settled," she said, and looped an arm through Nick's like he was escorting her into a grand ballroom. Nick had to admit, he didn't mind.

They made their way down the hill on 161st from Grand Concourse, crossing Walton and Gerard, going past an electronics store and the McDonald's on River Avenue, then passing underneath the green subway platform until the Stadium came into view.

"What does *your* dad think about all this?" Nick said.

"You want to know the truth?" Marisol said. "He thinks what's going on is terrible."

"Which part?"

"All of it," Marisol said.

Then they were swept along by a sea of Yankees fans as they inched closer to one of the Stadium's entrances.

Nick's dad had promised they would see Michael Arroyo pitch in person at least once during the season. Now Nick felt a little guilty, knowing it was due to Marisol's dad that he was seeing Michael Arroyo pitch. But the tickets had come from Michael himself, albeit indirectly, and Nick knew his father would have gotten a kick out of that.

The seats were amazing, as Nick knew they would be, having checked out the view from the virtual seat map of Yankee Stadium online. He knew his dad would never have been able to afford the crazy price for seats like these. Few people could.

Here he and Marisol were anyway.

That's the crazy part, Nick thought. *We're here.*

Then all of the anticipation that had been building inside Nick reached its peak when a great roar emanated from all corners of the Stadium. The cheers were for Michael Arroyo, who had come jogging onto the mound, preparing to throw his first pitch to the Red Sox leadoff hitter.

When Michael threw a fastball past the guy for strike one, the noise only got louder.

"This is awesome!" Marisol screamed into the crowd.

"No," Nick said, in awe. "It's *way* better than that."

Michael struck out the side in the top of the first. When he came off the mound and walked toward the Yankee dugout, the fans behind the dugout, including Nick and Marisol, stood and hollered and waved to get his attention. Michael looked up into the stands and tipped his cap as a way of acknowledging the cheer.

"Oh my God!" Marisol said. "It's like he looked right at us."

"I *know*," Nick said. It was the closest he ever felt to Michael Arroyo.

For the rest of the game, Nick watched every move Michael made. He saw him set up for each pitch on the third-base side of the pitching rubber. He observed how Michael shortened the stride with his front leg whenever there was a runner on base, not that there were very many, even for a powerhouse batting order like the Red Sox had.

Nick noticed when he threw breaking balls ahead in the count. He saw how many fastballs Michael threw at ninety-eight and ninety-nine miles per hour, and even a few that clocked in at a hundred. He also saw how Michael wasn't afraid to throw his changeup, even when he was behind in the count.

"It's even better watching him in person, isn't it?" Marisol said.

"Oh yeah," Nick replied.

Nothing could compare to this.

"I don't know what's more fun," Marisol said. "Watching him, or watching you watch him."

It turned out to be a great game, as the Red Sox starting pitcher matched Michael scoreless inning for scoreless inning. Finally, though, the Yankees broke through with two runs in the bottom of the seventh. At that point, it looked as if Michael would get through the top of the eighth. But when he gave up a two-out single and walked his second batter of the game, the Yankee manager came out to get the ball, and signaled for the Yankees' closer to come in and try for a four-out save.

Michael walked into one more ovation as he came down the dugout steps, waving his cap to the crowd before disappearing from view.

The night had been everything Nick imagined it would be. For the past two and a half hours, he was able to escape from his own world and live inside Michael Arroyo's for a change.

Marisol had been taking most of the pictures, while Nick zoned out, entirely focused on the game. The last one she took was of Michael waving his cap. She showed it to Nick and said, "Found your new laptop screen."

With two outs in the top of the ninth and the Yankees still leading 2–0, Nick turned and saw Marisol's dad kneeling in the aisle.

"Soon as our closer gets one more out," Officer Pérez said, "you guys need to come with me before everybody starts to leave."

Nick felt a twinge of disappointment. He wanted to stay through the final play of the game. "Where are we going?" he asked.

Officer Pérez smiled, and looked more like Marisol than ever.

"There's somebody who wants to meet you," he said.

35

As they walked quickly up the aisle from Section 114, Officer Pérez handed them credentials with "Yankee Guest" written on the front, and told them to hang them around their necks.

"I feel like we've got backstage passes at a concert," Marisol said.

"Yeah," Nick said. "A baseball concert." *Whatever is taking us away from the game will most definitely be worth it*, Nick thought.

Finally, the game let out, and hordes of people came flooding from each section. It felt as if they were swimming upstream. Officer Pérez pulled them through a door in the area behind home plate, past an elevator, and down some stairs that opened into a long hallway. They could still hear echoes of all the people above, but it was much quieter where they were. Along the way, Marisol's dad pointed out the interview room and the Yankee clubhouse right across.

They walked past the clubhouse and continued down the hallway before Officer Pérez told Nick and Marisol to stop.

"What do we do now?" Marisol asked her dad.

He grinned.

"We wait."

"For who?" Marisol said.

Nick thought he knew. Was *hoping* he knew. But was afraid to ask.

Don't tell anybody your wishes.

"Just wait," Officer Pérez said.

Then he walked back in the direction of the Yankee clubhouse, leaving Nick and Marisol tingling with excitement.

"Are you thinking what I'm thinking?" Marisol said.

"Yes," Nick said.

"But I shouldn't say it?"

"Don't you dare."

They waited in the hallway for what seemed like forever, and were startled by the sound of a golf cart whizzing by with two men sitting inside it. Nick's heart raced at the sight, but then the cart was gone and the area underneath Yankee Stadium where they were standing was quiet again.

Nick's chest was easing back to normal when he saw Marisol's eyes go wide. She stared past his shoulder, and Nick heard a pair of voices.

Officer Pérez was coming back down the hallway.

With him, wearing a gray Yankees T-shirt and his uniform pants, was Michael Arroyo.

36

WHEN MICHAEL REACHED THEM, HE SPOKE TO MARISOL FIRST.

"Heard a lot about you from your dad," he said, reaching a hand out. "You're the tennis star."

Marisol took his hand and shook it. "I don't know about that," she said shyly.

Nick thought, *At least she's able to talk.*

"Your dad certainly does," Michael said, lightly elbowing Officer Pérez.

Then Michael turned to Nick. "And you must be Nick García, the star pitcher."

Michael stuck his hand out and Nick shook it firmly, hoping Michael wouldn't notice how clammy and shaky it was.

"And I don't know about that, Mr. Arroyo," Nick said, riffing off Marisol's answer. *Thank goodness she went first*, Nick thought.

"Call me Michael," Michael Arroyo said.

"Okay," Nick said, looking up at his idol.

Michael smiled. "I hear you can really bring the heat," he said. "You know, they used to say the same thing about me when I was your age."

"I do know," Nick said.

I know everything about you.

Nick thanked Michael for the tickets and congratulated him on the game he'd just pitched against the Red Sox. Tonight's win put the Yankees a game ahead of them in the standings, with not much of the season left in the American League East.

"I was hoping to go the distance tonight," Michael said. "Get myself another complete game."

He looks taller in person.

"I thought the home-plate ump squeezed you a little bit on that walk," Nick said.

Just standing here talking baseball with Michael Arroyo.

"Right?" Michael said.

Then Michael shocked Nick by asking him how the Blazers were doing. Maybe Marisol's dad had clued him in to Nick's team's name, but either way, it was nice of him to take interest. Nick told Michael they were still undefeated, moving up on the championship game.

"Which I hear you're going to pitch," Michael said.

"Hope so."

"Man," Michael said, "is there anything better than pitching the big game in Little League?"

It wasn't lost on Nick that the Yankees' starting pitcher was nostalgic for his Little League days. Even with all the fame and success that came with being a professional baseball player, there was still nothing that compared to playing with your buddies under the lights.

After a bit more chitchat about the Blazers and the Dream League, Nick was thinking Michael probably had somewhere else to be. He was about to thank him again for the tickets when

Michael turned to Officer Pérez and Marisol. "Could Nick and I have a moment alone?" he said. "I want to talk to him about his letter."

"My letter?" Nick said.

"The one Officer Pérez gave me," Michael said. "About your dad, and pretty much your life story."

"But I didn't—" Nick stopped there, then tried again. "How . . . ?" He turned and looked at Marisol.

"You go talk to Mr. Arroyo about the letter," she said. "We'll talk later."

Michael placed a hand on Nick's shoulder, and they walked far enough down the hallway to have some privacy. "I want to figure out a way to help you," he said finally. "What you wrote was really powerful."

Nick's brain was working overtime. How did his hero, Michael Arroyo, get ahold of his letter, the one he'd never shown a single person?

"It hit home with me," Michael said, "because I remember what it was like for my brother and me to grow up scared. And that's a lousy way to grow up, at least when you're not playing ball."

"It's gotten lousier since I wrote it," Nick said. Michael listened as Nick explained how the rest of the story had played out for his dad.

"Do you have a phone?" Michael asked when Nick finished.

Nick reached into the back pocket of his jeans and sheepishly handed his phone over to Michael. He was embarrassed by how outdated it must have looked to him. But all Michael did was take it from Nick and quickly punch out a number, holding it to his ear until it was clear somebody on the other line had picked up.

"Carlos," Michael said. "I'm with Nick García, the boy who wrote the letter." Nick knew Carlos was both Michael's older brother and his manager. "In the morning, I want you to start figuring out what we can do to help Nick and his dad."

Carlos must have asked if something happened, because Michael replied, "ICE has him now."

He listened and said, "Mr. Gibbs from child services was there for us, Carlos. We gotta find a way to help this kid."

Michael ended the call and handed Nick back his phone.

"My brother likes to get things done," he said.

Nick beamed. "I've got a sister like that."

The last thing Michael said to Nick was this:

"I won't forget about you."

Nick, Marisol, and Officer Pérez were outside the Stadium now. On their way home, Marisol regaled Nick with the story of how the letter fell into Michael Arroyo's hands.

"Your sister found it open on your laptop screen," she said. "Then, when you told her about tonight's game, and how my dad knew Michael, she had the brilliant idea to ask if my dad could pass the letter along."

"So you read it, too?" Nick said to Marisol.

"Yes," she confessed. "And as soon as I did, I knew Amelia was right. We had to do something."

"I can't believe this," Nick said, still trying to process it all.

"Believe."

Nick turned to Officer Pérez as they were passing Joyce Kilmer Park.

"But if you knew what was in the letter," Nick said, "why didn't you arrest my dad?"

Officer Pérez smiled. "Nick, my job is to lock up bad guys. Your dad isn't one. And never was."

"Thank you, sir," Nick said, grateful to hear the words from someone who understood the law.

"Don't thank me," Officer Pérez said. "Thank Marisol. And thank your sister when you see her."

"Oh, I plan to," Nick said.

They walked Nick to the front of his building, but before he went inside, he said to Marisol, "So you and Amelia teamed up."

"We might not be as good a team as the Blazers," she said, raising an eyebrow, "but you have to admit, we don't stink."

37

"You passed my letter to Marisol," Nick said to Amelia when he walked through the door. She was sitting on the couch watching one of her shows.

"That is correct," Amelia said.

"You saw what I'd written on my laptop that night and decided to print it out." He should have been angry. Should have been horrified that his private, personal thoughts were made public without his permission. But had Amelia not done what she did, he may have never met his hero. And his hero would never have known about their circumstances and offered to help.

Amelia bit her lip, holding back a smile, and looked as if she were about to burst. Nick hadn't seen her so happy in weeks.

"I believe I might have mentioned something to you about firing up a prayer," she said.

She had a blanket over her legs, which were swollen again today, just not as bad as before.

"I still can't believe you did it."

Amelia giggled. "To tell you the truth, neither can I."

He sat down at the other end of the couch.

"It still doesn't mean they'll be able to help any more than Mr. Gasson can," Nick said.

"But Carlos is a lawyer, too," Amelia said. "And two lawyers are better than one."

"Yeah, two lawyers and one Major League Baseball player."

Nick leaned his head back on the couch cushion and rested his eyes. Their mom had gone to bed early tonight. Graciela García never complained, but both her children could see how exhausted she was when she got home.

"I still feel guilty that I'm playing ball while Dad's cooped up in that place," Nick said. "There's gotta be a better use of my time."

"You're the one who brought Mr. Gasson into our lives," Amelia said.

"And you brought in Michael Arroyo," Nick said.

His sister poked him in the ribs. "No," she said. "You did that on your own. I just delivered the message."

Nick heaved himself off the couch.

"Where you going?" Amelia asked.

"To write about my night," he said. "Though this time, I think I'll be more careful not to leave it where others can find it." He winked at Amelia.

"Would you have believed a few weeks ago that a night like tonight was even possible?" Amelia said.

Nick shook his head. "Never."

"Then maybe anything still is possible."

Nick wanted to believe she was right. Since the beginning of the Dream League tournament, Nick had held tight to his dream of throwing out that first pitch at Yankee Stadium.

Now he had bigger ones.

Much bigger.

38

IT WAS OFFICIAL: THE CHAMPIONSHIP GAME, IN ONE WEEK, WOULD come down to the Blazers against Eric Dobbs and the Giants. The Blazers' last game before that was this Saturday, against the Tigers.

Nick was able to speak to his dad on the phone before he left for Macombs Dam Park. He knew how painful these conversations were for both of them, but it was better than the alternative of not getting to speak at all. Each conversation was the same. His dad seemed farther away than ever, which made Nick miss him even more.

"I just want you to come home," Nick said.

"It is all I want, too," Victor García said. "We just have to trust in God, and Mr. Gasson to build his case."

By now, Nick and his family knew what that case was: that Victor García was a good man, leading a respectable and honorable life in America, and should get a bond hearing as soon as possible. They would argue to release him from the detention center in New Jersey until the case could be heard in front of an immigration judge, even though that might not happen for another two or three years.

There was so much more Nick wanted to say to his father, but their calls always ended too soon. Tonight, Victor García steered the conversation to Nick's game against the Tigers.

"You pitch your best tonight," his dad said.

Nick grumbled, "Coach might not even let me start."

"Doesn't matter," his dad said. "Even though I won't be in my seat in the bleachers, I'm here for you in spirit. You know that, right?"

Nick swallowed hard. He could feel the tears welling up, feel his throat starting to tighten.

Be strong, he told himself. *Like him.*

"I'll win for you," Nick said.

"No," his dad said. "You win for yourself and your team."

He told Nick he loved him.

"I love you more," Nick said before hanging up the phone. Then he walked over to his bed to pack his duffel. He threw in his bat and glove and water bottle.

Plus one more item: Victor García's old catcher's mitt.

It was as close as Nick could come to having his dad with him at Macombs Dam Park.

"You can pitch as much or as little as you want tonight," Coach Viera told Nick when he and Ben arrived at the field. Diego was already there warming up.

"Fine," Nick said. "I'll go all seven innings."

"You know I meant that you can pitch as much as your pitch count allows," Coach said. "But if it were me, I'd want to save my arm for the championship."

"I'm not coming out just to get ready for next Saturday," Nick said. "I've got the whole week to rest up. And, Coach? It feels like I haven't pitched in a month."

"But if you feel tired," Coach said, "I want you to say something. You've got a lot going on right now."

Coach knew about his dad. By now, everybody on the team knew.

"I won't get tired," Nick promised.

"I just don't want you to wear yourself out for a game that won't affect the standings."

"It will affect whether we're undefeated going into the championship, though," Nick said.

Coach grinned.

"Okay, then," he said. "Good talk."

As Nick and Ben ambled over to the warm-up area, Ben said, "I still can't believe you and Michael Arroyo are boys now."

"Yeah, right," Nick said. "He's going to start hanging out with us and Diego."

"Let's do the math," Ben said. "If you make it to the Yankees at the same age *he* was when he made it to the Yankees, you two might pitch together someday at Yankee Stadium."

Nick stopped.

"I'm just gonna say this to you," he said. "Right now, I'm not thinking about pitching *for* the Yankees. Just pitching in *front* of them in a couple of weeks."

"We're just two starts away," Ben said, reaching up with his mitt for Nick to tap with his own.

It was hard for him to wrap his brain around the fact that he only had two starts left in the Dream League. They were so close to the end, and it had all happened so quickly. Even with all that had transpired off the field, Nick had enjoyed the ride with Ben and Diego, Coach Viera, and the rest of the Blazers. But after what Michael Arroyo had said, about there being nothing like playing in Little League, he wondered if he'd allowed himself to enjoy it enough. There were no guarantees in life, he knew that by now. So there were no guarantees about how many baseball summers there would be like this.

But he promised himself that he was going to appreciate the two Saturdays he had left in the league. Because who knew when he might have another chance to play on this field, in the shadow of Yankee Stadium.

His mom was here tonight. So were Amelia and Marisol—the new dream team. Even Mrs. G came along, which Nick was not expecting. The second he saw her sitting next to Graciela in the stands, he ran right over to greet her.

"I'm part of the team now," Mrs. G said.

"Yeah you are," Nick said, and gave her a warm hug. "An honorary Blazer."

Then it was time for the first pitch of the game. Nick walked the Tigers' leadoff hitter on four pitches, not missing by a lot, but feeling more rusty than anything else. So he stepped off the mound, turned his back to the plate, and rubbed up the baseball just as a way of collecting himself. Then he struck out the next two guys and got the Tigers' cleanup hitter to hit a slow roller to Darryl at first base.

When he and Ben met back up at the bench in the bottom of the first, Ben said, "A couple of those fastballs you threw were as hard as you've thrown all year."

"You felt it, too?"

"Yeah," Ben said, "I felt it," then showed Nick the red mark on his left palm for proof.

The Blazers scored two runs in the bottom of the first, and

two more in the second. By then Nick had given up his first hit of the game, a clean single from the Tigers' pitcher, Nelson Avila. He'd thrown a good pitch and Nelson had gotten his bat on it and that was baseball. But Nick knew how good the ball felt coming out of his hand tonight. Knew how loose and free he was throwing. This *was* the best fastball he'd had all tournament.

Before Nick went out for the top of the fifth, Coach told him it would be his last inning.

"Figured," Nick said.

"You could call it a night now, if you want."

It wasn't meant as a threat. The Blazers were winning 7–0.

"You really think that's what I want?" Nick said.

Coach gave him a smirk. "I withdraw the comment," he said. "Just go finish in style."

Nick struck out the Tigers' second baseman on three pitches.

Then he did the same with their catcher.

As his teammates threw the ball around the infield, Nick and Ben caught each other's eye, the two of them having a silent conversation.

They both knew.

One more strikeout, and he would pitch his immaculate inning: nine pitches, three strikeouts.

The hitter was the Tigers' center fielder, Tommy Diaz. Nick poured a fastball past him for strike one.

Nick did it again with his second pitch, with Tommy swinging under it. Strike two.

Ben stood up and fired the ball so hard back to Nick that Nick thought it might leave a mark like Ben's.

But Nick knew the message behind the throw: Ben wanted this as much as Nick did.

Nick took a deep breath. Nodded at Ben. Went into his motion, not rushing anything, not letting his body get too far in front of his arm, and threw the best fastball he'd thrown all night or maybe all year, a high strike but a strike all the way, and Tommy swung under that one, too.

Three up, three down.

Nine pitches.

All strikes.

The game wasn't over yet, so the only celebration Nick allowed himself was a quick punch into the pocket of his old glove as he walked off the mound.

When the game was over, Ben made sure to collect the game ball for Nick. As he handed it over he said, "It's like they say in that Nike commercial about LeBron: it's only crazy till you do it."

Nick peered at the ball and saw that Ben had already gotten a pen from somewhere and written the date on it. Later, when he got home, Nick placed the ball next to some of his trophies on the shelf above his desk.

He washed up and settled into bed, pulling the covers around him. But something made him get up again. He switched on his desk lamp, reached up to the shelf, and took the ball down. He turned it over once in his hand, felt the seams with the tips of his fingers, and looked down at the date.

And not understanding why, unable to stop himself, *now* he began to cry.

39

MR. GASSON STOPPED BY THE APARTMENT THE WEDNESDAY BEFORE the championship game.

Nick knew the Bronx Defender had plenty of other clients besides Victor García to worry about, but today he told them he was working to get a bond hearing scheduled for Nick's dad.

"I'm trying to get us on the calendar as soon as possible," Mr. Gasson said, "so we can explain to a judge why your dad should go back to living his life for the time being. That's only until we can get him in front of another judge and make our plea to grant him freedom to live in the country permanently."

"Do you think you can?" Nick said.

"I can't promise anything," he said. "But it's happened in the past."

"So you're saying there's a chance," Amelia said.

"Do you think you might hear something by the end of the week?" Nick asked.

"I know I'm the lawyer here," said Mr. Gasson, "but your guess is as good as mine."

Then Nick's mom had a question. "How many of these cases come out the way you want them to?"

"Not nearly enough," Mr. Gasson said. "But enough to keep me going."

He stood up.

"You know how I look at it?" Ryan Gasson said. "Like I'm fighting for our country, in a war we have to win."

Nick and Ben and Diego were at the field bright and early Saturday morning, even though the game wasn't scheduled until six o'clock at night. The field looked good as new, as if the season were starting all over again. The grass was freshly mowed, the lines had a new coat of white paint, even the infield dirt looked brand new. Or as new as dirt could look.

"We can come here tomorrow morning," Diego said. "It just won't be the same."

"Not with the season over," Nick said. "All it'll feel like is the end of summer."

"It kinda is," Ben said. "We start school the week after next."

"Noooooooooo!" Diego moaned.

"Seriously?" Ben said. "I can't believe our baseball season ends tonight."

"Nah," Nick said. "For us, baseball season *never* ends."

There was a Yankee game scheduled for one o'clock that afternoon, but Michael Arroyo's next scheduled start wasn't until Sunday. Ever since Michael had used Nick's phone to call his brother, Carlos, Nick had been hoping for a call or a text message with an update.

But there had been no call, and no messages. Mr. Gasson said he'd spoken to Carlos Arroyo on the phone the night of the Yankees–Red Sox game, but hadn't heard from him since.

Nick and Amelia had been talking about it at breakfast that

morning. Their mom had already left for work. She'd found herself an extra job in Manhattan to make up for the income they lost without Nick's father's paycheck.

"It's not as if Michael and Carlos are supposed to be Bronx Defenders, too," Nick said to Amelia. "I mean, Michael *is* kind of busy trying to help the Yankees win another World Series."

"But he's the one who said he'd be able to help," Amelia said.

"He said he'd *try* to help," Nick clarified, feeling a need to defend his hero.

Amelia shrugged. "Maybe they should try harder."

"You don't know that they aren't trying," Nick said. "Either one of them."

"And you," she said, "don't know that they are."

Nick saw the look on her face, and knew there was no point in continuing the conversation any further. Their parents weren't the only stubborn ones in the family.

"They should *all* be trying harder!" his sister said, her voice wavering, and she pushed away from the kitchen table, chair screeching against the floor, and walked out of the room.

At that point, Nick grabbed his duffel and headed out to meet Ben and Diego at the field.

40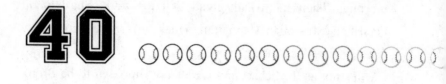

At about five minutes to six, Coach Viera gave them their last pregame speech of the tournament.

"What we're all experiencing right now, this minute, are the best parts of being on a team," he said. "This feeling is one you *only* get from being part of a team. It means you've gotten the most out of yourself and have seen your teammates do the same."

The Blazers were seated in the grass on their hill behind the field, together like this for the last time. Coach stood in front, but farther down the slope, looking up at his team.

"You guys are exactly where I expected you to be when this tournament started," he said. "Every one of you has done everything I've asked, and more."

Now he stuck his hands in the back pockets of his jeans and smiled.

"There's a famous basketball coach, Pat Riley, who once said there's only winning or misery," Coach said. "But I myself have never thought of sports that way. Win or lose tonight, nothing can take away the memories we've made or the fun we've had."

Now he motioned for everyone to get up and gather around him. He put out his right hand about shoulder high, and the Blazers reached in to pile on top.

"Now all that's left is to go out and make one more memory," Coach Viera said.

They walked down the hill together. Ben on one side of Nick, Diego on the other, the memory beginning a few minutes early.

Eric Dobbs avoided making eye contact with Nick during both teams' pregame warm-ups. Nick knew Eric was cocky, but he still wasn't sure he understood the attitude. Maybe Eric thought, because his dad worked for the Yankees, he deserved to throw out the first pitch, as if Yankee Stadium were his real home field. Clearly, Eric was peeved not to be a shoo-in for MVP already. Nick was his biggest competition, but there were others in the league who could give Eric a run for his money. Big Benny Alvarez, for instance, had hit home runs in every Dream League game except the one against the Blazers, the night he collided with Nick.

Ordinarily, Nick would run over to wish the other team's starting pitcher luck before the game, as a way of showing good sportsmanship. But this time Nick stayed away from Eric and Eric stayed away from him. He didn't forget what Eric had said in the handshake line after their initial game: "Next time." So Nick didn't see the point in trying tonight.

"Think that's his game face?" Diego said, nodding at Eric before the Blazers took the field.

"Nah," Ben said. "I think that's just his face. He goes through life looking like he just sucked a lemon."

"Or maybe he thinks he's too good for us," Diego said.

"He's probably still mad we're his only loss of the season," Nick said.

"One more loss than you have," Ben said. "Just sayin'."

"Let's keep it that way," said Diego.

Nick let out a breath. "I just have to remind myself this isn't a game of one-on-one."

Ben poked him with an elbow and grinned. "Isn't it, though?"

Nick's cheering section had grown since the last game. His mom and Amelia were there with Mrs. G, along with Marisol and her dad, wearing street clothes tonight instead of his uniform.

As a surprise, Mr. Gasson showed up, too. He sat next to Officer Pérez.

Carlo Rotella, the Giants' shortstop, led off the game for his team. Nick struck him out with fastballs. José Barrea, the catcher, was batting second. He hit a slow roller to Kelvin, playing second tonight, and Kelvin threw him out easily.

Eric Dobbs came to the plate.

Ben set up inside. Prior to the game starting, he'd told Nick they were going to own the inside of the plate tonight, not allowing any of the Giants hitters to get too comfortable. Nick came inside now, a little more than he intended. It wasn't his way of sending a message to Eric or moving his feet. But he did anyway. Eric jumped back as the home-plate ump called ball one.

Eric glared at Nick before getting back into the box.

Nick thought, *He's acting like I buzzed him even though the ball didn't come anywhere close.*

Whatever.

Game on.

He came back with a fastball on the outside corner that Eric waved at and missed. Two pitches later Eric badly missed a high fastball that probably would have been called a ball if he'd let it go. Strike three. Inning over. Nick sprinted off the mound and back to the bench.

Ben sat down next to him. "You're already inside his head."

"With one inside pitch?" Nick said skeptically.

"Yup," Ben said. "And by the end of this game, we might be *living* inside that head."

"Rent free," Diego said.

But Eric could still pitch. It was nothing but a pair of goose eggs on the scoreboard after three innings. In the top of the fourth, Nick struck out Eric with two runners on base, then got two more strikeouts to end the inning.

The game stayed 0–0.

It was everything a championship game should be. Every pitch mattered, every swing, every base runner. They knew the longer the game stayed scoreless, the more important the first run would be.

It was Nick, batting third tonight, who finally gave the Blazers their best chance of getting on the board in the bottom of the fourth. Through three innings, the Blazers had only one hit, a single by Ben in the first inning. But with one out in the fourth, Nick crushed the first pitch he got between the Giants' center fielder and left fielder.

By the time the ball made it back to the infield, Nick was standing on third with a triple. For some reason, a quote from Astros manager A.J. Hinch popped into his head. He'd once said, on the night his team was about to be eliminated by the Red Sox in the playoffs, "We've got to fight a little bit of the anxiousness that comes from being behind in an elimination game."

Nick wanted to give the Giants that kind of anxiety, the same as if they were playing Game Seven of the World Series.

Nick wasn't a pitcher now. Just a runner trying to get home, any way he could. It didn't matter whether he scored on a hit, an error, a passed ball, or a wild pitch.

He just wanted to score.

Coach Viera took a couple of steps toward Nick from the third-base coaching box.

"Be ready for anything," he said into Nick's ear.

"Anything" happened on Eric's first pitch to Ben.

Eric tried to put too much on it and bounced the pitch at least a foot in front of the plate. The ball ricocheted off José Barrea's chest protector and up the first baseline before he could get ahold of it.

"*Go!*" Coach yelled.

Nick was already on the move.

He saw José come to a sliding halt when he caught up with the ball, and Eric running for the plate as hard as Nick, matching him pace for pace.

Nick knew he had him beat by a very slim margin.

From their very first practice, Coach had warned Nick never to slide headfirst, to avoid landing on his pitching shoulder or getting his hand stepped on. So he went in feet first, his body halfway across home plate when the ball hit Eric's glove.

The ump had already yelled "Safe!" when Eric slapped a hard tag on Nick.

Right across the face.

Nick's head snapped to the side, and he immediately cupped his jaw in pain.

"What the heck?" Ben yelled from where he stood a few feet away.

Eric was hovering over him, and somehow Nick managed not to bump him as he got to his feet.

"You did that on purpose," Nick said, taking a step back.

"Just trying to make a play, dude," he said, grinning. "Got a problem with that?"

Nick was about to say that he *always* had problems with dirty plays and dirty players, but swallowed the words before he could. It wasn't worth the risk of getting thrown out of the game.

Ben came onto the field then, and tugged Nick in the direction of the Blazers' bench. Eric was heading back toward the mound when he muttered, "It's not like I did anything *illegal*." He stepped pretty hard on the last word. "You know about illegal, right, García?"

Nick jerked to a stop, and Ben tightened his grip around him.

"What did you say?" Nick said.

"You heard me," Eric said, tossing up the ball casually with his pitching arm.

"Let it go," Ben whispered as Nick took a step back in Eric's direction.

"That's enough conversation for one night," the umpire said, getting between them. "Now let's get back to playing ball."

"He's just trying to get inside *your* head," Ben said when they were back on the bench.

"Felt more like he was trying to knock it off," Nick said, touching a palm to his cheek.

Darryl's mom ran over and handed Nick an ice pack from her cooler. She instructed him to hold it to his face until it was time to go back out and pitch.

It was Ben's turn in the batter's box. The count was already two-and-oh, and then Eric came down the middle with a fastball and Ben hit what the announcers on TV called a "no-doubter," to dead center field. The ball went hard and fast over the head of the Giants' center fielder before he even turned to chase after it.

Ben was already rounding third base by the time the kid ran the ball down. He intentionally took his time, jogging toward home, glaring at Eric as he crossed the plate.

Diego high-fived Ben in the on-deck circle, and all the Blazers swarmed around excitedly, patting Ben on the back and rustling up his hair.

Ben plunked down next to Nick on the bench, breathing hard but smiling.

"When you say you've got my back," Nick said, "you're not messing around."

"Less talking," Ben breathed. "More icing."

"How do I look?" Nick said, taking the ice pack away.

"A lot better than Eric feels."

"Seriously, does it look bad?"

He pulled the ice pack away.

"Maybe only to your girlfriend," Ben said.

"She's not my girlfriend!" Nick said, so loudly he was sure Marisol must have heard him in the stands.

Diego doubled then, and Darryl singled him home. The Blazers were ahead 3–0. Nick played a dream inning in the top of the fifth. Sometimes you didn't need strikeouts, just outs, and fast ones. He threw five pitches total for the inning, getting two ground balls and a short pop fly to Diego in center. His pitch count didn't suffer for it.

Nick didn't say anything to Ben, or Diego, or Coach, but he'd made up his mind to go the distance tonight. It was his last game in the Dream League, and it could be the last he played on this field or in the Bronx. He was going to finish what he'd started.

Nick made his case before the top of the sixth and Coach listened.

"Okay," he said.

Nick balked. "Really?"

"Really," Coach said. "But don't think I won't take you out if I see you struggling out there. The object of the game is to *win* it."

"You know I know that."

Coach put his hand on Nick's shoulder. "Go win us the championship."

Nick got a strikeout and two more grounders in the sixth. The game was still 3–0 with three outs to go, and Nick knew exactly where the Giants were in their batting order.

If he got two outs to start the top of the seventh, the last batter he would face this season was Eric Dobbs.

Nick struck out Carlo Rotella on four pitches.

He did the same with José Barrea.

Then Eric Dobbs stepped into the left-hand batter's box.

Nick didn't come inside this time. Just right at him. Eric swung and missed.

Missed badly.

He stepped out, took a deep breath, stepped back in.

Nick threw another fastball, and Eric was late.

Again.

The count was oh-and-two.

One more, Nick thought. Just him and the ball, Ben and his mitt, and baseball.

He threw Eric another fastball—more high heat—and Eric missed that one even worse than the first two.

Blazers 3, Giants 0.

Ball game over. Tournament over. But not the end of the night, and far from the end of Nick's story.

After the game was over, all the Dream League coaches gathered around the mound with some of the league coordinators to vote on the MVP. They'd announce the winner right after presenting the championship trophy.

Nick sat on the Blazers' bench with Ben and Diego on either side, waiting. They watched Coach with all the other coaches conversing in hushed tones, huddled together to have their conference.

"It has to be you," Ben said.

"I don't want to talk about it," Nick said, but his hands were trembling.

"Dude, I get not wanting to talk about it during the season," Diego said, "but if there was ever a time to talk about it, it's now."

"It has to be you," Ben said again.

Nick knew it wasn't a done deal. "Benny hit a gazillion home runs," he said.

"But we won the championship," Diego said, bouncing on his heels.

Practically everything had come out right this season, for himself, for Ben, for Diego, for their teammates.

Control what you can control, he thought.

But in the end, he had no control over this.

He inhaled slowly, trying to get his heart rate down to normal as the coaches came walking back toward the infield.

He searched Coach Viera's face for any indication of good news, but Coach was all business, averting his eyes, careful not to look over to where Nick, Ben, and Diego were sitting.

The championship trophy sat on a table near the pitcher's mound. There was no trophy for MVP. The trophy was the first pitch. The trophy was Yankee Stadium, right across the street.

One of the league coordinators stepped up to the microphone that was set up next to the table and presented the Dream League championship trophy to the Blazers. Diego went running onto the field first, followed by his teammates, and they hoisted the trophy above their heads in celebration. Cheering and hollering and patting each other on the back. Nick joined them, but he couldn't let go completely. Not with the MVP decision still up in the air. After about a minute or so, the noise abated as the Blazers ran back to their bench.

Then the coaches designated Coach Viera to speak on their behalf, so he shuffled to the front and stepped up to the microphone. A single speaker was set up alongside it. Coach tapped the mic a couple of times to check if it was still working.

"I don't know if everybody here knows it," Coach finally said when he had everyone's attention, "but the MVP of our Dream League will have the opportunity to throw out the first pitch at Yankee Stadium. It's at the discretion of the coaches to select an MVP, and I'm thrilled to say the decision was unanimous."

Nick held his breath and sat on his hands to keep them from shaking.

"The Dream League, in association with Major League Baseball and the Yankees franchise, is proud to announce," he said, "that Nick García of the Blazers hasn't thrown his last pitch of the season."

41

NICK'S MOM INSISTED ON HAVING A PARTY BACK AT THE APARTMENT.

"We're going to celebrate," she told Nick. "Our home has been quiet for too long. For one night, we are going to be surrounded by people and noise and fun."

They picked up pizza and ice cream on the way home. Marisol and Officer Pérez followed them back to their apartment, as did Ben, Diego, and their parents.

And Mrs. G.

Mr. Gasson accepted the invitation, too, and somehow managed to get Nick's dad on the phone from New Jersey.

"Heard you got smacked in the face," Victor García said.

"Yeah. But I'm still thinkin' it hurts less than losing a championship."

First thing Nick did when he got home was check his face in the bathroom mirror. The ice had helped. There was swelling, of course, but it wasn't as bad as he'd anticipated.

When Nick came out of the bathroom Ben said, "You might have a bit of a shiner in the morning."

"I took a pretty good shot."

"A *cheap* shot."

Nick shrugged. "Still shook Eric's hand in line."

"I forgot to ask," Ben said. "What did he say?"

"'Good game.'"

"Guy still can't get it right," Ben said, shaking his head. "That wasn't just a good game you pitched. It was a *great* game."

The apartment was charged with excited energy. While they ate, everyone talked about the game, pointing out various highlights and notable plays made by Nick, Ben, and Diego. Inevitably, the conversation turned to a different topic, the one regarding Nick's MVP award and the first pitch at Yankee Stadium. It was surreal for Nick to be talking about it out loud after so many weeks of secrecy. But now that it was official, a sense of relief washed over him. More than that, this particular window of time between the MVP announcement and the first pitch brought on a kind of exhilaration Nick hadn't felt in years. It was the satisfaction of achieving a dream mixed with the anticipation of fulfilling your destiny, and Nick wished he could live inside it forever.

Toward the end of the night, before everybody left, Mrs. G got up and sang a song from one of her favorite operas, called "Must the Winter Come So Soon." She sang it so beautifully, it made Nick's mom cry.

Afterward, Marisol leaned over to Nick on the couch and said, "You're lucky to have so much love in your life."

Nick nodded. "I just need a little more."

"Love?" she said.

"Luck."

The guests gradually said their goodbyes and thanked Graciela for hosting them.

Mr. Gasson was the last to leave. He said he wanted to give

them an update on Victor's status, even though there wasn't much new to report. He still hadn't been given a date for a bond hearing.

"So nothing's changed," Amelia said, making no attempt to hide her disappointment.

"I'll just keep preparing our case for when our time comes," Mr. Gasson said. "Part of it involves your medical condition, Amelia. When I get my chance, I'll explain to the judge that the best treatment you can get can only be found in the best city in the world."

It made Amelia smile. "Glad we can put lupus to good use for a change."

A tangible calm settled over the room then, in stark contrast to all the noise and liveliness of the party. They sat together on the couch.

"I know it's like this unspoken thing," Nick said. "But the conditions in the detention center are awful, aren't they?"

"I don't want to lie to you," Mr. Gasson said, though it pained him to be so candid, "but the facilities are not what I'd deem satisfactory."

Nick shifted uncomfortably. It was the answer he expected, but not the one he wanted to hear.

"It would take a miracle for him to get to Yankee Stadium, right?"

"Miracles happen," Mr. Gasson said, urging Nick not to lose hope. "And if I can make one happen, I will."

They thanked him again before he left, and then Nick figured he'd better get to his laptop while the night was still fresh in his mind. It was important to get the details down exactly right so he'd never forget a single moment.

Because of his misgivings at the start of the season, it wouldn't have occurred to Nick to expect this day to arrive. He hadn't given thought to how he'd feel if he won the MVP award; never gave himself permission to imagine it. Yet here he was, preparing for one of the most important events of his life. Doing it all without the one person he'd hoped to share it with: his dad.

Nick wrote it all down with no intention of showing it to anybody. He was careful to save it in a hidden folder on his desktop so there was no chance of anyone discovering it. Not even Amelia.

If he didn't tell anybody, the wish could still come true.

That's how it worked, right?

42

FOR THE NEXT FEW DAYS, NICK CALLED MR. GASSON RIGHT AROUND lunchtime to check for an update, holding out hope that somehow his dad might still make it to Yankee Stadium.

Mr. Gasson explained how he was taking a new approach with the deportation officer assigned to Victor García's case. It was possible he could get Nick's dad released into custody just for one night, to see Nick throw his pitch.

"It's another long shot, Mr. Gasson said. "But it's not unheard of to release a detainee for special circumstances like weddings or funerals or graduations. I'm trying to convince them that your dad ought to be able to see a once-in-a-lifetime opportunity for his son."

Ten days went by like ten minutes, and suddenly it was the day of the pitch. Nick hadn't heard from Mr. Gasson yet, but he wasn't ready to let go of his belief that miracles could still happen.

They arrived at the Stadium in the early evening, about an hour before the game was scheduled to start. Nick, with his mom, Amelia, Ben, Diego, and Marisol as his own personal entourage. The first thing Nick did when he arrived was leave a ticket for his dad at will call.

Just in case.

He left another for Mr. Gasson.

A woman named Debbie from the Yankees' promotions department was waiting for them near Gate 4. She welcomed them and walked them through security into the Stadium. Coach Viera and the rest of the Blazers would be showing up later; their seats were right behind third base. After Nick threw out the first pitch, he would be sitting right next to the Yankee dugout with his family and friends, in the richest seats the Yankees had.

Debbie asked if Nick would be all right throwing to the Yankees' catcher, but Nick asked if he could throw to Ben instead.

"We're kind of a team," he said.

"Fine with me," Debbie said, jotting it down in her notebook. "The optics will be terrific."

"Optics?"

"Just two young guys having a game of catch at the most famous ballpark in the world."

Debbie pointed to what Nick had in his hand.

"I see you've even brought a catcher's mitt for Ben."

"Actually, it's my dad's," Nick said.

Debbie's brows furrowed. "Is he coming?"

"Hoping he's on his way."

"Oh, so he's coming from work," Debbie said.

Nick looked down at his feet. "Not exactly."

Then he checked his phone. It was 6:15. He was throwing out the first pitch just before seven o'clock, ten minutes or so before the first pitch of the game between the Yankees and the Tampa Bay Rays.

He said to Debbie, "I hate to ask for anything . . ."

"Ask away," Debbie said. "It's your night."

"My dad would be coming from New Jersey," he said. "If he gets here in time, would it be all right if he was the one catching my pitch?"

"Well now," Debbie said, "that would be a *dream* optic, wouldn't it?"

You have no idea, Nick thought.

He turned to Ben, hoping he'd understand if, at the last minute, Nick's dad filled in as catcher.

"I've caught every pitch you've thrown all season," Ben said. "But trust me, this one time I'd be happy for Mr. García to take my place."

Debbie had one of her assistants show Graciela, Amelia, Marisol, and Diego to their seats in the first row, while she led Nick and Ben past the visitors' clubhouse and down an entranceway out to the field. They came out on the third-base side of Yankee Stadium.

The stands weren't nearly full yet, but Nick didn't care. He and Ben stood gazing out at the field, soaking it all in at once: the bright green of the turf practically glowing under the white lights projecting out, the crisp blue of the outfield walls, the huge screen in center field flanked on both sides by various advertisements. Then, out where he knew all the monuments and plaques were exhibited in Monument Park, the most famous museum in baseball outside of the National Baseball Hall of Fame in Cooperstown, New York.

Out here, Nick didn't have to check his phone. There was a big clock in the outfield.

It was 6:40.

Still time for his dad to make it somehow.

Not much.

But still.

If Mrs. G was right, and this was the way his story was supposed to end, then Victor García should come running onto the field any minute.

Announcers always talked about how one of the charms of baseball was the absence of a clock. But right now, Nick felt as if he were trying to beat one.

Debbie excused herself to handle some official Yankee business, leaving Ben and Nick to admire the field. They stood with their feet planted, marveling at their surroundings and thinking of how crazy it was that they were here.

Eyeing the front row, where his mom, Amelia, and Marisol sat, Nick noticed Diego wasn't with them and pointed it out to Ben.

"Where do you think he is?" Nick said.

"Knowing him?" Ben said. "Probably getting ice cream."

"Hey!" Diego shouted from behind them. "You should know I wouldn't have ice cream without eating a hot dog first."

Nick and Ben turned over their shoulders to see Diego standing beside Debbie at the entrance to the field, the hot dog in his hand smothered in ketchup and mustard.

"I was told," she said coyly, "that the three of you are a team. Didn't think tonight should be an exception."

Now they each stood there, taking in the sights and sounds of Yankee Stadium together.

Diego looked to Nick and Ben. "Think they'd mind if I ran out to center field?"

"Uh, *yes*," said Ben.

Nick just rolled his eyes. Classic Diego.

He'd hoped to see Michael Arroyo on the field, but it was getting close to game time, and he was probably in the locker room suiting up. Since their conversation several weeks prior, neither Michael nor Carlos Arroyo had reached out to Mr. Gasson.

Nick had to face facts. No matter how good their intentions were, maybe there was nothing they could do to help his dad.

In the end, though, Michael was still his hero, and Nick still wanted him to see his pitch from the Yankee dugout.

He checked the clock again.

It was 6:50 now.

He squinted into the stands where his mom was, noting the empty seat beside her, still imagining the scene playing out the way he'd written it, with his dad running down the aisle . . .

But then Debbie said, "It's time."

Time. All Nick needed was a little more time. Debbie walked him and Ben toward the pitcher's mound as the voice of the Yankees' public address announcer came over the speaker.

"Tonight's first pitch will be thrown out by twelve-year-old Nick García," the voice echoed through the Stadium, "the Most Valuable Player for the Dream League tournament that concluded last week, cosponsored by the Yankees and Major League Baseball."

Nick took one last look over at the first row.

The seat next to his mom was still empty.

"He's not here," Nick said to Ben. His dad should've been on the field by then, ready with his catcher's mitt, crouching behind home plate.

"But you *are*," Ben said, pulling Nick back into the moment. He left Nick on the mound and walked in the direction of the batter's box.

Then Debbie handed Nick a brand-new baseball. Looking down, he saw that it had already been signed by Michael Arroyo: *For Nick, who will someday pitch from this mound for the Yankees. Your friend, Michael.*

Nick angled his head toward the Yankee dugout. And there Michael was, standing on the top step, smiling, pointing at him with both hands.

Nick went and took his place on the rubber. The mound felt so much higher than the one at Macombs Dam Park, as if Nick were standing on top of a mountain.

But even here, in the great baseball place, things got quiet for Nick. He blocked out the rumble of the crowd so that all he could hear was the beating of his own heart.

He took one last look around, absorbing every last detail. This part of the dream looked almost exactly as he had imagined it would. Almost.

Nick looked in at Ben. No mask on him tonight. Nick could see the big smile on his face, as he set Nick's target with Victor García's glove.

Then, for the last time this season, Nick brought the heat.

THREE
MONTHS
LATER

43 ⚾⚾⚾⚾⚾⚾⚾⚾⚾⚾⚾

I T WAS THE FIRST WEEK OF D ECEMBER, A LITTLE OVER A MONTH
after the Yankees had won another World Series.

Officer Pérez had gotten Nick and Marisol tickets to Game
Six, so they were lucky enough to be there in person when
Michael started and won the deciding game.

Now, almost four full months after Victor García was taken
to New Jersey, came what Nick and his mom and sister hoped
would be a different kind of ending. After all this time, Victor still
forbade his family from seeing him at the detention center, wearing his orange jumpsuit like a common criminal, in the terrible
conditions Mr. Gasson described. Nick could never decide
whether it was pride on his father's part, or anger, or shame, or
all those things combined that made him so insistent his family
never come visit.

But today, they would get to see his face at least, on the large
monitor that was set up in the courtroom of the immigration
judge. The one who would preside over Victor's bond hearing,
here at the courthouse on Varick Street, near the Holland Tunnel.

They'd be able to see Victor García even if the only people he'd
be able to see through the screen were the judge, Mr. Gasson,
and the ICE attorney appointed to his case.

It wasn't long after Nick and his mom and Amelia had taken

their seats in the spectator area, a row behind Mr. Gasson, that Victor's face popped up on the screen.

"My Victor," Graciela García said softly.

Amelia, looking pale and tired—likely from the hour-and-a-half-long subway ride it took to get there—reached over and grabbed Nick's hand.

Soon they would find out if their dad would be released from custody, free to officially petition for what was called a "cancellation of removal," as in removal from the United States.

Mr. Gasson kept reminding them that the process could take years, and that thought made Nick's head swim. For now, he tried to stay clearheaded on what they all wanted to see happen today: the judge ruling in favor of his dad coming home.

Today it was up to Mr. Gasson to control what *he* could control.

At last, a door at the back of the courtroom opened, and the judge, an older man wearing round spectacles and a black robe, walked in and took his seat at the bench, calling the hearing to order. He gave Mr. Gasson the floor to proceed with his case.

Mr. Gasson presented the judge with all of the letters of support he'd collected for Victor García: from both the owner and the manager of the restaurant where he worked, a few of Victor's other colleagues, and some friends and neighbors in the community who knew Victor García's character well. Mr. Gasson presented Amelia's medical history into evidence, and Victor's tax records as well.

"Yes, Your Honor, Mr. García pays his taxes," Mr. Gasson said. "He believes it is the American thing to do. Another misconception about noncitizens is that they don't pay their taxes. But Mr. García does."

Mr. Gasson sat at a table across from the judge and continued to speak about Victor García's life in New York, and why he'd chosen to stay in the city after his tourist visa expired.

"He was afraid that if he left he would never be allowed to return," Mr. Gasson said. "This wasn't criminality, Your Honor. This was a young man driven by the dream of a better life than the one he had left behind."

Mr. Gasson explained that Nick's dad had only jumped the turnstile that day out of desperation. He couldn't risk losing the chance at a good paying job, something that would have allowed him to further acclimate to American life. He went on to describe the truth behind the fight in front of the urgent care clinic, how the man attacked Victor on a night when he was preoccupied with his daughter's health.

Mr. Gasson spoke for a long time.

Then it was Victor García's turn.

He appeared much thinner than the last time Nick had seen him. And the four months he'd been away seemed to accelerate his aging. He looked older and even grayer than Nick remembered.

But he was still his dad. A man of few words even now, with his freedom on the line.

"I have made mistakes, Your Honor," Victor García began. "But those mistakes do not change the fact that the only thing I love more than this country is my family. I have tried to honor them, and America, through my work ethic and by the way my wife and I have raised our children, how we've taught them to dream. The way I myself have lived the immigrant dream so many before me have lived."

The ICE attorney spoke next. He was a bald man in a gray suit, who sat at his own table facing the judge. He argued, in what Nick thought was an unnecessarily cruel way, why the government believed Victor García should remain in New Jersey. He pointed out that Victor had now broken the laws of the land on three separate occasions: when he had originally overstayed his visa, when he had jumped that turnstile, and when he had gotten into the fight in front of the hospital. He didn't stop there, accusing Victor García of being a threat to the community and a strain on America's resources, before adding that having a sick daughter didn't change or excuse these facts.

"We don't make these laws, Your Honor," the ICE attorney said. "It is simply our job to ask that they be enforced. Frankly, Mr. García believes he's honoring his country by only following the laws he likes, and ignoring the ones he doesn't. America doesn't work that way, at least not for Americans who actually respect our country's laws."

Nick looked down and saw his own fists clenched, the way his dad's had been that night in front of urgent care. The night that had started them on the road to this room. The ICE attorney was making his dad sound like a dangerous man, someone who should be locked up and kept away from society. He was twisting the story to serve his own purposes. But then, Nick knew he should have expected this. Mr. Gasson warned them they weren't going in without a fight. The ICE attorney was bringing his case, same as Mr. Gasson. That's how the legal system worked. Nick just had to be patient and hope the judge found their case to be the stronger one.

The judge then gave Mr. Gasson the opportunity to respond. For some reason, Mr. Gasson looked at his watch and turned toward the door to the courtroom. Nick thought he looked upset about something, or annoyed, but couldn't figure out why.

"Yes, sir," Mr. Gasson said, clearing his throat. "I do have a few more things I'd like to say to the court."

"I am not only here to speak on Victor García's behalf today," he said as he lifted himself out of his chair. "I speak for all those like him, who were drawn to the possibilities of America, who came here in search of a better life, whose stories are as American as yours or mine. The true greatness of this country can be found in its history, a history written by immigrants like Mr. García. He isn't a flight risk. He isn't a danger to his community. He is a proud and productive member of that community, and should be able to return to it, and his family, tonight."

He turned toward Nick and his mom and sister and gave them a weak smile, a message to hold on and keep hoping.

"It's worth remembering today how our national anthem concludes, 'the land of the free and the home of the brave,'" Mr. Gasson said. "Victor García is brave, Your Honor, as brave as anybody I know. It is time to finally set him free."

Nick wanted to stand and cheer, but stayed fixed in his seat as the judge said, "Is there anything else, Mr. Gasson, before I make my ruling?"

Mr. Gasson took one last look at his watch, and then back at the door, before shaking his head.

"No, Your Honor."

Mr. Gasson was about to sit down on his side of the chamber when the door to the courtroom creaked open.

Through it walked Michael Arroyo.

44

"I'M SORRY I'M LATE, YOUR HONOR," MICHAEL SAID. HE WAS WEARING a tailored navy-blue suit, and it took Nick a minute to recognize him without his Yankees uniform. But when he did, his mouth hung open in shock. "I've lived in this city a long time, and still never account for all the traffic."

"Nor do any of us," the judge said, chuckling.

"My name is Michael Arroyo."

The judge's lips turned up into a smile. "I know who you are," he said.

"Your Honor, I'd like to now call Michael Arroyo to the stand to testify in support of Mr. García's request for bond," Mr. Gasson said.

The ICE attorney didn't object. The bailiff swore in Michael, and he sat down at the bench.

"Please tell us in your own words about your relationship with Mr. García," Mr. Gasson said.

Then Michael Arroyo began to speak about having come to know Victor García after visiting him at the detention center in New Jersey. Nick's eyes went wide in disbelief when he heard that. Mr. Gasson happened to be looking over at him at the time and gave Nick a wink.

"Victor's son, Nick, is already a friend of mine," Michael said, "a baseball child of the Bronx the way I was. We both understand loss, though in different degrees. My dad was taken from my brother and me when he died of a heart attack. Now Nick's dad has been taken from him."

Michael looked over at Mr. Gasson.

"Are you supposed to ask more questions?" he said.

Mr. Gasson grinned. "You're doing fine on your own."

Michael told the story of his own childhood then, about how his dad had risked everything to get to America, taking his sons on a dangerous boat ride across the Florida Straits from Cuba. He spoke of how his father had suffered a fatal heart attack while trying to break up a fight on a New York City sidewalk. And how afterward, he and his older brother lived on their own, with the fear of the government threatening to break them up.

"But the government didn't separate us," Michael Arroyo said. "It didn't just allow my brother and me to live out our dreams, but to live out my father's dream of America, the one for which he risked everything, and gave everything. They kept what was left of our family together, and that's really all Mr. García is asking: for his family to remain together in America."

Then it was the ICE attorney's turn. If he was a Yankees fan, he didn't show it. His expression hardened. "Despite your dramatic appearance here today, this isn't a baseball game, Mr. Arroyo."

Michael grinned. "Thank you for pointing that out."

"Do you really expect this court to believe you have actual knowledge of Mr. García after only meeting him once?"

"I do," Michael said flatly.

"And how is that?"

"Because he reminds me of my own father," Michael said. "He didn't just wear his heart on his sleeve. He wore his honor."

"Do you follow the laws of this country, Mr. Arroyo?"

"I do."

"Do you think everybody should?"

"I do," Michael said. "But I was also raised to believe there can be a difference between the spirit of the law and the letter of the law. And by the spirit of the law, Victor García is a good man, not a criminal."

"Maybe you're just used to people agreeing with everything you say," the ICE attorney said, acting almost insulted that anybody in the room would disagree with him.

"Or maybe you are, sir."

Nick was sure he saw the judge crack a smile.

"Victor García is a criminal," the ICE attorney stated.

"Is that a question?" the judge said.

"I'll rephrase," he said. "Are you aware that by the laws of this city and country, Mr. García is a criminal?"

"What I believe is criminal, sir," Michael said, "is having this man locked up and separated from his family. Maybe you think that's the America you should be representing. But it's not my America. And not the one my father dreamed about in Cuba."

They went back and forth like that for a few minutes longer. But the attorney couldn't shake Michael or make him lose his temper. Nick pretended the ICE attorney was swinging and missing at each fastball Michael Arroyo pitched him. Finally, after the questioning was completed, Michael left the stand and

walked past Mr. Gasson, before taking a seat in the row behind
Nick. He leaned forward and whispered, "I told you I wouldn't
forget you."

Nick whispered back, "Talk about bringing the heat."

There was a brief fifteen-minute recess while the judge delib-
erated. Then he returned to the courtroom, stepping up to the
bench. The image of Victor García came back up on the screen,
and the judge announced he had reached a verdict.

Nick held his breath, and Michael placed a hand on Nick's
shoulder from behind as extra support. Amelia held his hand,
and their mother held hers. This was the moment they'd waited
for, and yet it was terrifying all the same. Whatever happened,
they would face it together, as a family.

The judge cleared his throat and read some legal information
about the case off a sheet of paper. Then he peered out at the
courtroom over his glasses.

"Mr. García will be released from the detention center in New
Jersey as soon as he posts a five-thousand-dollar bond," he said.

Nick couldn't restrain himself. He'd never cried happy tears
before, but his face was wet with them. Amelia's, too. They stood
up and hugged each other tight, but when they turned to their
mom, she was still seated.

A single tear drifted down Graciela García's cheek.

"We cannot afford that kind of money," she said, almost in a
whisper.

Nick's heart sank. Then, from behind them, Michael Arroyo
said, "But I can."

The judge said that court was adjourned, and a few minutes

later they were all standing outside on Varick Street. First Nick's mom, then Amelia, then Nick thanked Mr. Gasson for everything.

"You never gave up hope," Nick said.

"And neither should you," he said. "I told you miracles can happen."

Then Nick turned to Michael Arroyo.

"I don't know how to thank you," he said.

"I ought to thank you," Michael said. "Sometimes it's easy for me to forget the boy I used to be. You've helped me remember."

"We still have a long fight ahead of us," Mr. Gasson said. It was true. This was only the first step on their journey.

Nick looked up at Michael. "But we're on a winning streak now, right?"

Michael winked in reply. "See you at the Stadium," he said.

Then he stepped into the back seat of a black SUV waiting for him at the curb. Before long, the car was pulling away from the courthouse, and then Michael was gone.

45

A LITTLE AFTER NINE O'CLOCK THAT EVENING, AFTER MICHAEL HAD sent his car to New Jersey to pick him up, Victor García walked through his front door. He was home.

Nick was in his arms first, followed closely by Amelia, and then Graciela stepped in and closed the circle, her and Victor's arms enveloping their children in a long embrace. There was such a commotion, they were sure even Mrs. G could hear downstairs. Tonight, as she predicted, their story ended the way it was supposed to, at least for now.

"As happy as we all are in this moment," Victor said after he finally pulled away, "you know this is really more of a beginning than an ending, right?"

"We know," Graciela said, taking her husband's hands in hers. "But that doesn't mean we can't enjoy it for the time being."

"It's just important for all of us to keep in mind that we have a long way to go, and there are no guarantees."

"Dad," Nick said. "We're not going anywhere."

For a brief moment, Nick thought his dad, as tough and brave as he was, was about to cry.

"This is still a crazy dream," Victor said, wiping his eyes.

Nick smiled. "Only until it happens."

Turn the page
for a sneak peek of

PROLOGUE

ALL I WANTED WAS TO PLAY FOOTBALL.

This is what happened because I tried.

1

ALEX'S FATHER DENIED IT EVERY SINGLE TIME SHE'D ASK.

"I know you wanted a boy, Dad. It's okay, I get it," she'd tease.

They were having the conversation again, on their way to the Orville town fair in western Pennsylvania. They'd spent the afternoon at the Pittsburgh Steelers training camp in Latrobe, a couple of towns over.

"How many times do I have to tell you?" Jack Carlisle said to his daughter. "You were exactly what I wanted. It was almost like I ordered you from Amazon Prime. Free shipping and everything."

"Then answer me this," she said. "Why'd you give me a boy's name?"

Jack Carlisle breathed a deep sigh. "Your mom and I *didn't* give you a boy's name," he said. "We named you Alexandra. You're the one who wanted us to call you Alex."

Alex smirked at her dad from the back seat. She never tired of messing with him like this. And despite the sighs and head-shakes, she knew he loved it, too. It happened a lot when they were together. And they were together all the time. Jack Carlisle and Alex's mom had divorced when Alex was only four. Her mom moved to the West Coast to become a surgeon and remarried, leaving Alex and her dad in Orville. Alex had regular phone calls with her mom, but she was closest to her dad. They were two

2

peas in a pod. They both loved sports, but they loved each other more.

Alex's dad was a Steelers fan through and through. He followed other sports, too. Just not as closely as football, and not with the same enthusiasm as he rooted for the Steelers. When Alex was around eight years old, her dad began to notice how much she loved running and catching balls, and throwing them most of all. He used to joke that sports were one of the few things he'd passed on to his child. That, and his piercing blue eyes.

Nevertheless, Alex was still convinced he'd wanted a boy. And she told him so now in the car.

"I'm a lawyer, and I can't even argue with my own daughter," he said, shaking his head like he did when the Steelers were forced to punt.

They were stopped at a light now. He used the brief pause to turn to Alex in the back seat and said, "You know how much I love you, pumpkin pie."

He had a lot of nicknames for her, so many that Alex lost track of them all. But "pumpkin pie" was the first one she could remember.

"I do," she said, giving him a playful wink so he knew she was joking. "Admit it, though. You would have loved me a *little* more if I were a boy."

He sighed, resting his forehead against the steering wheel. "Alexandra Carlisle."

"Call me Alex," she said, and her dad chuckled. She loved making him laugh. It made her feel as if she'd scored a goal in soccer or struck out a batter in softball.

They'd had a great day at Saint Vincent College watching the Steelers practice. Now they were heading back to Orville, because Jack Carlisle had promised to take Alex to the fair. Her dad had told her about a famous Steelers wide receiver, way back in her grandpa's time, named Jimmy Orr. Jack Carlisle explained that their town wasn't named after Jimmy Orr, but probably should have been.

It was already the third week of August. The Steelers were playing preseason games, and Alex knew that the National Football League now had strict rules limiting the number of contact drills between games. But that was fine with her. She enjoyed watching all the passing drills, particularly the amazing accuracy of the three Steelers quarterbacks, from the shortest handoffs to the longest deep throw. She never got tired of watching the running backs and receivers run their patterns with such precision, making their cuts to the inside and outside from almost the exact same points on the field.

More than anything, Alex loved watching the flight of the ball, perfect spirals finding their way to their intended targets.

At one point her dad asked her if she was getting bored.

"Are you serious?" she said. "This is my team in front of me. It's *our* team."

"It'll be better when they start playing season games," Jack Carlisle said.

"Yeah." Alex nodded. "And we're back at Heinz Field."

Her dad had a pair of season tickets to Steelers games, on the thirty-yard line, visitors' side of the stadium. Jack Carlisle said he liked it better over there, because the Steelers coaches and players would be facing them, even from the other side of the field. One ticket for dad, one for Alex. They went to two preseason games and eight regular season games every year. Then, fingers crossed, to a home playoff game or two after that. The preseason games took place in August, and even though the quality of play wasn't much, the weather was usually pretty nice. Toward the end of the season, though, western Pennsylvania could feel colder than Alaska.

Even so, Alex and her dad never missed a game.

Loving the Steelers was one of the things that bonded Alex and her dad. They were as close as a father and daughter could be, and Alex could never imagine loving anybody or anything as much as her dad.

"My football girl," he called her, and not just during football season.

The Orville fair was set up on the grounds of the local church. They'd parked their car in the lot, bought tickets, and walked under the balloon archway at the entrance. Now they made their way across the fair, the sun still high, with plenty of daylight left before they'd have to head home for dinner. Seventh grade for Alex wasn't starting for a couple more weeks. She knew all her friends were trying to milk those last precious days of summer vacation and dreading the first day of school. But not Alex Carlisle. The start of the school year meant that the start of the NFL season was just around the corner. Pretty soon, she and her dad would have their Steelers back. Alex was always a little sad when they broke camp at Saint Vincent, just because the college was so close to where they lived. It made her feel as if the Steelers were practically *living* in her neighborhood. Heinz Field, on the other hand, was more than an hour away.

Alex still liked football better when the games counted, no matter how many times her dad took off work to take her to training camp. She liked her own sports better when the games counted, too. Softball in the spring, soccer in the fall.

Soccer was supposed to start up the week before she went back to school. Alex was a good enough player. She was a right backer, which meant she mostly played defense. Everybody talked about her passing and her vision and her decision-making.

She was a good, solid player.

But Alex wanted more than that from sports. From anything, really. She didn't talk about her dreams much. Didn't talk about them at all, in fact. Not even with her dad.

But her biggest dream was this:

Alex Carlisle wanted to be great at something.

Her favorite teacher at school, her English teacher, Ms. McQuade, always said the greatest adventure of all was the journey to finding your passion.

Alex hadn't found her passion yet.

Oh, she knew she had a passion for football, and for the Steelers. But that was different. No matter how much you loved your team, you were on the sidelines watching them. From the stands or the sofa.

You weren't in the game.

Yeah, she told herself. *You are good at soccer. Really good. But not great.*

The previous year, Alex and her teammates had watched together as the United States women's team won another World Cup. She had secretly rooted harder for the star player she considered her namesake, Alex Morgan. Her passion was clear. So was Megan Rapinoe's.

Alex Carlisle wished she could feel that way about soccer. And as good of a pitcher and hitter as she was, she didn't feel that way about softball, either. Neither sport was her dream. But she had a dream all right. It was just out of her reach. Like trying to grab a star out of the night sky and pull it down from the heavens.

"Hey," her dad said. "Where were you?"

"What?" Alex said, pulling herself out of her reverie.

"I felt like you left me there for a second," he said. "I asked what you want to do next."

"Oh," she said. "Sorry. It's like you always say: my head was full of sky."

"So what *do* you want to do?"

Alex put her hands on her hips and looked around, getting a panoramic view of the place.

Then she spotted the coolest and biggest stuffed animal she had ever seen in her life. But not just any stuffed animal . . .

"I want you to win me Simba!" she said.

The Lion King was Alex's favorite movie of all time. She loved the original animated version and watched it over and over to the point where she had the whole thing memorized. When the new live-action movie came out, she had dragged her dad to the Orville Cinema the day it opened for the midnight screening. They went back three or four times after that. One day she hoped to see the Broadway musical in New York City.

Of all the characters, Simba was her favorite. She thought Simba was the bravest. But more than that, Simba's story resonated with her. It took him a while to realize his own dream, about being king. Just like Alex was taking time to figure out hers.

Alex's love for *The Lion King* rivaled even her love for the Steelers.

"Dad," she said, tugging on his arm, "come on. You've *got* to win me Simba."

They'd already been to a booth where you tried to win prizes by tossing softballs underhand into a milk crate. That didn't quite pan out for Alex and her dad. They'd stopped at the dunk tank, where Jack Carlisle hit the buzzer, plunging one of Orville's high school seniors into the water. The students were raising money for a local charity, so it was for a good cause.

But in the next booth over, where Alex spotted Simba, you had to toss a football through a hole that looked barely wide enough to fit, well, a football. The odds were unfavorable, to say the least. On the wall, an image of a football player was painted with his arms up, as if receiving a pass. The hole was where the hands came together.

Jack Carlisle had once been the starting quarterback at Orville High. He wasn't good enough to play college ball at Penn State or the University of Pittsburgh. But he'd had enough of an arm to lead the Orville Owls to the league championship in his senior year.

"I've got no arm anymore," he said to Alex. "Heck, when

we're playing catch in the backyard, you throw better than I do."

Alex knew he was right about that but didn't want to discourage him from trying to win her the enormous stuffed animal. It would take up the whole back seat of her dad's car. It was amazing. She couldn't leave the fair without it.

Jack Carlisle made a beeline for another carnival game, but Alex grabbed his shirt sleeve and pulled him back toward the booth.

"Come on, Dad," she said. "Aren't you always telling me the most important thing for a quarterback is hitting what they're aiming for?"

"Yeah, when you've still got the arm," he said. "I left mine back in high school."

"You've still got it!" she said. "Who'd know better than your favorite wide receiver?"

"I've still got it *in the backyard*," he said.

"Please, Daddy," she said, looking up at him with big, pleading eyes. She knew she was being dramatic, but it was fun to tease him.

"Oh, here we go with the *please, Daddy*," he said. "I'm assuming that'll be the same tone of voice you use when you want your own car someday."

"Today I just want a lion," she said.

It cost five dollars for three throws. The young man running the booth said that nobody had put a football through the hole since they'd opened that morning.

Now that they were standing at the counter, Alex understood why. She was pretty good at judging distances. This was at least a fifteen-yard throw from where they stood. Maybe even a little more. She looked at the hole, then over at Simba, and thought:

Really big prize.

Really small target.

"You got this," she said to her dad.

"In your dreams," he replied.

Alex smiled.

If he only knew.

Her dad made a big circle motion with his right arm, giving himself a quick warm-up. He groaned as he did.

"Nobody likes a whiner," Alex said to him.

Her dad huffed at that. "You better hope I don't pull a muscle," he said, "or you'll be driving us home."

"Really?"

"No," he said, laughing.

The young man handed Jack Carlisle a beat-up-looking ball from a basket of them on the counter and grinned.

"I don't want you to think I'm betting against you," he said. "But my shift ends in half an hour, and I bet one of my buddies twenty bucks that nobody would make this throw today. Nobody made it yesterday, either."

"You can start counting your money right now," Jack said.

"Hey!" Alex said. "A little positivity couldn't hurt."

"More like wishful thinking," he replied.

Then he took his first shot.

The throw missed the player completely. He groaned even more loudly than he had while warming up. "That was pathetic," he said.

"You said it, not me," Alex said, throwing her hands up in defense.

"Hey," he said, grinning. "Who's got the bad attitude now?"

His second throw hit the player.

In the knee.

"Getting closer," Alex said.

"That's your pep talk?"

Alex just shrugged, but flashed her dad a quick smile.

His last errant throw, to Alex's great amusement, hit the player right below the belt.

"Now *that*," the guy behind the counter said, "has *got* to hurt."

Alex couldn't help it. She laughed. Even though that last miss meant her dad had lost his chance at winning the prize.

"Oh, you think it's funny, hotshot?" her dad said, giving her a playful nudge. "Why don't you try?"

"You're willing to lose another five dollars?" Alex said.

"I've seen that arm of yours," he said. "Maybe I'm looking to *win* a bet. Even if it costs our friend here his."

"It's on," Alex said.

Her light brown ponytail was sticking out of the opening in the back of her black-and-gold Steelers cap. She removed it so she'd have a clear view of the target. Then she secured the rubber band on her ponytail nice and tight. She didn't warm up or anything. Just looked up at the guy behind the counter and held out her right hand, palm up. Asking for a ball.

He handed her one. She stepped back a few paces, making the throw about a yard longer. But that was so she could step into her throw.

She took a deep breath and exhaled slowly, smiling to herself. *I got this.*

Even though it *was* a regulation ball, it felt good in her hand. She and her dad always used a regulation ball in the backyard, and she loved the feel of the laces beneath her fingers.

Eye on the hole, she stepped into the throw.

Fired a perfect spiral right through it.

If it had been a basketball shot, the announcers would have said it hit nothin' but net.

The guy bent at the waist, hands on his knees. "Are you kidding?"

"My football girl," Jack Carlisle said to him, proudly slapping a hand onto Alex's shoulder.

Alex had shocked even herself. She hadn't expected the ball to go through, but it had. And maybe she could even do it again. Turning to the man in the booth, she put out her hand and said, "Another ball, please."

"You already won the prize," he said, incredulous.

"Yeah, but my dad paid for three throws," she said. "Gotta get our money's worth."

He handed her another ball, shaking his head. She took an extra step back this time.

The ball whistled through the hole again.

"Show-off," her dad said.

"How old are you?" the guy asked.

"Twelve," Alex replied.

"No way."

"Way," she said.

She put out her hand once more, and he tossed her the last ball. She fired another spiral right through the opening.

"Money," Jack Carlisle said.

"Not for me today," the man said in disappointment. He pointed toward the stuffed animals. "Which one do you want?"

Alex pointed to Simba. The guy used a grabbing stick to lower Simba off the wall of prizes and held it out to Alex. She received it as if he were handing her the Super Bowl trophy.

"You've got some arm for a girl," the young man said.

"I've got some arm, period," she said.

When they got home that night, Alex told her dad what she'd been keeping inside all summer: she wanted to try out for the football team at Orville Middle.

Read all of Mike Lupica's bestselling novels!